AF492557

It was a boring party, and I wanted to let everyone know I thought so. It wasn't hard. I made a fuss, pouted, told the girls to find something fun to do. They were mad, but I was right. Someone has to make sure we don't get boring. That was me.

A guy sidled up to me. "You're looking for something freaky."

"I could be, if it's cool."

He mimed taking out a cigarette. He didn't have cigarettes. "Like goats?"

"Do you mean, cool like goats, or do I like goats?"

He smiled. "Either. Look, pills." He held out a handful of little gold pills. "You can have one if you like. No biggie. They make you high all night."

"That's it?"

"Yeah. No hangover."

"And then it's *over*?"

He cupped his hands, produced an invisible lighter and lit the cigarette he didn't have. "Yeah, but then you have udders. They get bigger, for two weeks, and then you have nice big boobs, the same size as goats udders."

It was terrifying, but I was fascinated. "Okay. What's in it for you?"

"You'll be the girl with big tits. Every guy wants to know one girl with big ones."

He opened his hand and showed me a half dozen tiny red pills, and he looked at me.

I stared back. I didn't want to have anything to do with them, but I couldn't look away. I'd complained and he was calling my bluff. I knew if I refused I'd never see him again. I took a pill from his hand and crunched it.

It tasted worse than anything you can imagine. I washed it down with warm beer and didn't flinch.

He said, "Cool. See you round." He knocked off his ash that didn't exist and turned away into the crowd. I'm sure he did a dozen girls that night, or tried. Probably nobody but me was bored enough.

I was only bored for another minute, and then the world was hot and violent, and everything rushed past me and swirled away, and it all smelled wonderful and felt easy and good. I danced and laughed, and I woke up in my bed, and it was morning, and I still felt good.

And that was that. Nothing changed, and the next week was fun.

Maybe the drug stayed with me. I looked for the guy at other parties but he was gone.

By Wednesday my breasts were a little bit puffy. On Friday they felt solid and heavy, and they bounced when I walked. That was a shock. I've always been streamlined and skinny.

My friend Chloe told me I needed a bra. I didn't want to be that respectable, but she gave me an old one. Chloe is taller than me, but not much bigger around, and she has decent boobs, and it fit pretty well. They were more comfortable with some support.

On Sunday I put on a silk blouse that had fit me a week ago. My breasts squashed unevenly inside the fabric and pulled it tight across the front. I tried to adjust them through the fabric, but I couldn't. There must be some trick that busty girls knew. I tried not to think that I was one of them. My breasts stuck out too much, ridiculous, and so heavy I knew I had to do what I'd never wanted and go bra shopping. I bought a big black one with thick straps and learned to put it on. It wasn't easy, because I hadn't learned years ago, with small breasts. Girls looked at me differently, careful, and boys who'd used to be fun and cheerful treated me like dynamite, watched what they said, tried to be respectful. It was hard to have fun.

They were idiots. I had my own problems. In two days I was too big for the black bra, and my breasts bulged out of the cups. They wouldn't let me return it. Bras are expensive.

I'd been lithe and active and made my own fun, and suddenly I couldn't. I was too busty, and I wasn't used to it. I didn't want to be clumsy or to be surrounded by boys who wanted to wait on me, but I was. Girls I'd known forever looked at me with wary eyes.

My mother gasped and brought me a huge, solid bra, made from salmon pink nylon with stiff underwires. It was awful, industrial and ugly, and in the mirror it was huge and not at all stylish. Once I had it on it was heavenly and I couldn't be without it. My breasts stuck out in front of me like two traffic cones and my girlfriends made fun of me. I'd stopped being the skinny chick who could outrun all of them. I didn't care. I was comfortable. I hadn't known that mattered.

Three days later the pink harness was tight, and the next morning it wouldn't do up. It was like trying to stuff two mixing bowls of jelly into pair of teacups. I felt heavy and ungainly and I stayed at home. When I tried to do pushups my breasts squashed into the floor like pillows. I had to be halfway up before I couldn't feel my nipples touching the floor. It was cold. I pulled on a big t-shirt and lay in bed with a book. Every so often I'd look down at my shirt and wonder what was making it puff out like that. It was me.

The next day I shoplifted a bra. I grabbed one and stuffed it under my coat and bolted. I'd never been in that store, and now I could never go back. I thought that didn't matter, until I realized how few shops sell really big bras.

When I put it on my breasts didn't fill the enormous cups. I shortened the straps until they were snug, and it still didn't fit. I stayed at home again and read a book in the bath, my breasts floating, warm and weightless.

By the weekend the bra was loose and comfortable, and I spent Friday night sitting at a table letting boys stare at my boobs and buy me drinks. There was about a square foot of them you could see where my shirt wouldn't do up. I wanted to go out and do exciting stuff, but my friends had all deserted me. I wasn't the fun chick any more. I was the girl with big tits.

I made myself have a good time anyway. On Saturday the bra was a perfect fit, and on Sunday it was snug and my cleavage bulged out of it and looked stupid. I loosened the straps and made it to Tuesday. Then I sneaked out and threw it in the dumpster, wearing my best jeans and a t-shirt that had been empty and loose three weeks ago. Now it was stretched tight over my breasts, full.

That night I called Chloe. She said, "Huh. Talking to the common people?"

"Do you think I like this? I can't do anything fun for my boobs and a wall of boys." I held the phone with my shoulder and supported my boobs with both hands. That felt silly, and it was scary - I wasn't cupping them, just lifting them with fingers they hugely overflowed.

"Hm. So let's do something fun."

"Chloe, how big do goat's udders get?"

"I don't know. Let me look." I heard computer keys clicking. "This is those pills you took? That was stupid. Wow, you are so fucked."

I asked, "More than a handful?"

I could hear clicking. "Tits don't get that big. Well, these ones did. Wow, look at these chicks. They're like little cows with miserable expressions. Holy crap, this girl has even bigger ones."

"Chloe, you're not helping."

"I'm serious. How does she even stand up?"

"Chloe, I'm going to bed." I hung up. I read for a while, but it was hard to get comfortable. My tits were in front of me, too big to lie face down on, then lolling off to one side, huge and awkward. I got up and had a shower, cradling them in one arm so they didn't feel so heavy. Drying them was nearly impossible, and the skin under them stayed damp. I lay on my back on the bath mat and powdered them until they looked like floured bread dough. I walked back to my bedroom, holding each one in a hand. It was more comfortable to fold my arms under them, but they stuck out too far and jiggled when I walked.

Chloe knocked at the window. I jumped and yelped, saw who it was, and let her in.

"Wow, they're like whale's noses. Maybe their whole heads."

"Chloe, I'm already scared."

"That's okay. I brought you a gift."

It was a bra, bigger than the one I'd stolen. I bent over and eased them into it.

Chloe said, "Is that how you do it? I've always wondered how you big girls put them on."

"I'm not a big girl. This is a mistake."

"You could fool me.   I thought you had huge boobs."

I shuffled them into place. I was gloriously comfortable. In the mirror they looked ridiculous, too big for my chest. The cups were stiff and flesh bulged out of the cleavage, but I loved it. "Where did you get this? It's nice." I was an addict, and big ugly bras were my fix.

"My aunt has big ones, too. She's got dozens of them."

"Can you get me more?" I tried not to sound eager. I was planning ahead.

"Sure. Listen, I've been doing some research. Goats don't get that big."

"So?"

"Baby, I think that cut-rate shit you took was cow, not goat."

My stomach dropped. "Why?"

"Well, goats udders are kind of ... not like yours. How long did he say you'd grow for?"

"Two weeks."

"It's been three. And I did a web search. The research was all done on cows. Nobody likes goat milk."

I stared at her. "Chloe, I don't have milk."

"No, silly. But if you did, it would be cow's milk."

"If I did it would be girl's milk! I'm not a cow!"

"Don't be touchy. I'm sorry. Cows get veins on their udders. Goats do, too, but less so."

"So do people. And I don't have veins."

She took my fingers. "Feel there." She brushed them back and forth, tracing a heavy ridge that squashed away into velvety skin when I pressed on it. "You've got some serious vein action going. It's not ugly, but you've got them."

I was aghast. My breasts were small and light, not enormous bags of flesh with veins. "I have not!" I looked into the mirror. I wanted to take the bra off, but my breasts were heavy and they'd be uncomfortable. I was suddenly a girl who considered how long it would take to get out of her bra and put it back on. My breasts looked enormous and maternal. Veins covered the upper surfaces, a roadmap in pale blue.

"You can see them, can't you? Can you feel your nipples?"

"Of course." I fumbled for them. They'd been small and delicate, now they were huge, like wine corks.

Chloe said, "All I'm saying, girlfriend, is that whatever cows do to give milk, don't do it." She smiled. "I've got to go. I'll talk to Aunt Stevie about more bras." She poked my right breast and her finger sank in past the knuckle. She grinned and, and was gone, light and lithe, out of the window. I considered it with my new body image. I could probably scoot over the sill on my belly, but I'd get hung up on my breasts. I definitely couldn't do it without my bra on, but it would catch on the frame if I wore it.

My boobs stuck out in front of me, heavy and solid. The bra cradled them, pushing them up into wonderful cleavage, but when I looked in the mirror they were ridiculous, and they stuck out much too far. They weren't delicate and sexy, they were too huge to ignore, clumsily, immensely erotic. I was scared. I wanted to take off the bra and hide them in a baggy shirt, but they were too heavy, and they jostled and bounced, reminding me how stupid I'd been. Yesterday I'd put my bra on to walk to the bathroom. Now I wondered if I should wear one to sit in bed and read.

I walked into the bathroom and studied them in the mirror. The nipples looked like oversized teaching aids, surrounded by heavy blue veins, branching and curling, maybe elegant but thick and unmistakable.

Two days later I was too big for the bra. It wouldn't do up at all. When I looked in the mirror, wondering what to do, there were a lot more veins. Down in my cleavage were thick, pulsing ones, but the ones that showed on the upper surfaces were delicate and pale. I covered them with makeup. Chloe brought me a bigger bra. It didn't fit, but I forced myself into it. She apologized and promised to get another.

That night I lay on my front on a pile of pillows, breasts squashing out beneath me, bulging everywhere.

My nipples itched and I scratched them, my fingertips bouncing the rubbery flesh back and forth. Big breasts are fun to play with, and my nipples sent tiny bursts of pleasure up through my breasts, spreading and diffusing like fiery red ink dropped into water.

Skin has its own encoding system, an undocumented grid that tells you where you're being touched. Any sensation has an identity and a location, unmistakable. Mine was screwed up. When I cupped my nipples they swelled, filling my palms, but my breasts told me my hands were tiny. Fuck. They were growing faster than my body image could handle.

I spread my book open and put it upside down on the bedclothes, and sat upright. My breasts reared up in front of me, massive and soft, like bags of warm, thick cream.

I stood up. They were huge and heavier than they'd been, even yesterday, and I felt top-heavy and unsteady. I cupped them in my hands and crushed them against my chest, but they didn't squash that well, and my spread fingers weren't big enough to reach the bulging edges.

I walked into the bathroom, awkward and clumsy, and turned on the light with my elbow. The figure in the mirror was me, but with enormous protruding breasts and huge blunt nipples. I stumbled back to bed, horrified, and lay on my front, but my breasts bulged out under my ribs, too big, and I had to roll on my side.

I'd left my phone on the dresser, too far away to reach. I held my breasts, managed to stand up without using my hands, and grabbed it. When I was safely back in bed I called Chloe. "Get over here, now."

"I'm ready for bed. What's the matter."

"I'm freaking out. Come. *Please*."

Half an hour later she was sitting on my bed, while I leaned back on the pillows, breasts upright, my nipples pointing at the ceiling. My breasts felt impossibly sensitive. I could feel the air moving over them, eddying around my areolas.

Chloe said, "You've got yourself into some shit this time." She reached out for one. "Sorry, can I touch them?"

"Go ahead." I could tell when something touched them, but they were too big. They didn't feel like part of me.

She pressed her hand into the right one, flat, and watched it squash. "Holy fuck."

"You're not helping." But she was. I felt calm now she was here.

"Sorry." She fumbled in her backpack. "Here. I brought you another bra."

I stood up, clumsy, bent over and dropped my huge breasts into the cups. My nipples pressed into the pointed tips, first, and my breasts squashed them flat and filled the cups until they overflowed. "Crap. Chloe, they won't go in."

"Try again." She dug her hands in between fabric and flesh, making sure I was in. I felt like a domestic animal. A cow.

"Hmm. Stay there."

"They're awfully heavy."

"Just a minute." She loosened the straps and adjusted them. "That's all the slack you have."

I straightened up. The cups balanced on my breasts, held in place by thick straps, stretched taut. I bulged out around them but they supported me. I sighed. "That's a bit better."

She said, "What now?"

"You're supposed to tell me. I don't know. I can't wear a shirt. I'd look like a set of howitzers. I guess we go out tomorrow night like nothing has happened."

"Except you can't see over your boobs any more."

"Chloe, you're not helping."

"Sorry." She adjusted my right strap, and the whole breast shifted and wobbled. "I'm there for you, always. I just hope you're not going to get too much bigger."

"No." I couldn't say it, but I knew I was.

By the next night the bra was much too tight, but I didn't have
another one. I kept it on, and covered it with a shirt made from thick
black velvet. My nipples came erect as I pulled the soft fabric tight
across them, and they bulged out of the front, emphasizing my
already-enormous breasts. My reflection in the mirror looked
insane, impossible.

I couldn't button the shirt up as far as I wanted, and the bra shaped
my breasts into points inside it, leaving an air space big enough to be
drafty. When I looked down at myself the front of my chest was
bumpy and strangely shaped. I didn't care.

We sat in the back of the club where it was dark, and I rested my
breasts on the table. I'd been trying not to think about my huge
nipples and the veins that surrounded them, but when I went to the
bathroom I had to look in the wall of mirrors. Nothing else had
changed about me, but my tiny, pert breasts had grown into massive,
heavy cones, far too big to ignore. I tried not to say the word, even
to myself, but they were udders, huge and ungainly, and fast getting
bigger.

Chloe said, "Let's dance."

"Are you crazy? I can't sling these things around like that."

"Then dance gently. Come on." She took my hand and pulled me
upright. I secretly wanted to, so I followed her onto the dance floor.
It was dark and crowded enough that I wasn't too obvious, and I
managed a careful half-step that didn't shake my breasts too much.
It was fun, and I danced with a boy I liked. His eyes fell onto my
breasts a dozen times, and he dragged them back up to my face,
helpless. I couldn't tell him to tear open my shirt and crush my
nipples. I couldn't let him touch me, because no matter what he was
after, it wasn't udders. I didn't know what to do.

When the dance was over I returned to the table and ordered food.
I craved protein, and I gnawed a plate of chicken wings until the
bones were polished.

Chloe said, "I'm beat. Want to go back to my place and have a
pizza?"

"Sure." It sounded wonderful.

We walked slowly. I wanted to run but that would be clumsy and
embarrassing. I couldn't try with Chloe there. The cool night air
blew over the front of my shirt and my nipples stiffened, pulling

radiating creases across the front of my protruding breasts.

Chloe said, "Thinking about boys?"

"Always. Chloe, how can I let one touch *these?*"

"That's the boy's problem. I bet he'll manage."

"Yeah, but boys want boobs, not udders."

"That's not what I saw tonight. They were following you round the dance floor, panting."

That made me feel better. I felt hot, and I opened my shirt down to the last two buttons. The bra had shrunk again, and it pulled open, exposing my nipples. They felt cool and good.

Chloe said, "I know you like to be naked. Remember summer camp?"

"Oh." She'd seen me run down to the lake, nude, and dive in, high on moonlight and the air on my bare skin. She didn't know I'd done that every night, when the camp was dark and asleep, or how good it had felt. On an impulse I opened the last buttons and slipped off the shirt and bra.

"Wow." She admired them. "No bra?"

"No." In the dark I felt light and energetic, and my breasts were firm.

She ran her fingers over my left nipple, fanned out.

I inhaled, trying to be quiet.

"Shit. I hope you don't want a boy to suck on these. He'd never get one in his mouth."

"Chloe!"

Lights turned the corner a block behind us. She said, "Crap. Run."

She darted off and I followed, more slowly, my bust too heavy to let me run fast. The night air streamed over them, good, and I tried to speed up. I looked for Chloe and struggled past one house and another. I tried to steady my huge breasts but they were too big and I needed my hands free for balance. I held my arms out to my sides, fingers spread, desperate for their slight inertia. My hips wobbled, trying to compensate for the immense swaying weight of my breasts, but they still bounced and shook. I couldn't see the ground over them, and I stumbled over a curb and nearly fell, caught myself and kept going. My arms reached downwards and I took an extra step, my huge bust wallowing for a precious second, but I was okay. I felt my nipples shuddering, tautly erect. I couldn't see them.

The lights came closer, faster than I could ever have run. I dashed

between two houses, not caring how much I bounced and shook.
"Chloe?" I bent over, breathing hard, and wiped spit off my lips.
  "Right here. You looked great."
  The car slid past and vanished. "At least nobody saw."
  "And I got a movie."
  "You didn't!"
  "Come on, they might come back."
  A minute later they did. We ran again, and this time they were close enough for the lights to be blinding. I panted and my legs burned.
  Chloe said, "This way!" and dragged me into a yard with an open garage. The car slowed, then moved away.
  My throat burned, raw. I bent over, my hands on my thighs. "I'm going to puke." My breasts hung beneath me, huge pointed ellipses, slick with sweat. The nipples stuck out an inch and a half into the cold night air.
  "You'll get it on your udders."
  "Boobs, for fuck's sake." I took long, deep breaths until I felt better. My legs were shaky.
  "Follow me." Chloe led me across the street, checking for cars, and into a patch of bushes. "Can you put your shirt on?"
  I looked down at my chest. My hands were empty. "I don't know where it went."
  "Crap."
  We dodged from bush to bush, but the car didn't come back. Chloe led me down back alleys and across lawns under dark windows, staying out of the cones of light spreading under tall street lamps. A dog barked inside a house and my heart pounded, but nothing happened.
  Twenty minutes later we stood in the shadows beside Chloe's house, invisible. She pried open a window with her fingers and climbed in.
  It was at my chest level, and it looked easy. It wasn't. I was heavy and awkward again, and I couldn't use my hands to climb over the frame because I was holding my breasts.
  Chloe said, "Get inside before someone sees."
  "I can't. Let me in at the front door."
  I walked round to the front of the house, naked and hugely busty, my pale skin glowing white in the dark. She let me in and wrapped

me in a towel. I was pretty sure nobody had seen me. I felt safe inside.

Half an hour later I was in her housecoat, devouring an extra-large pizza with five types of meat, the best thing I'd ever eaten.

Chloe nibbled on a slice. She said, "I can almost see those things getting bigger."

"Hush." I was sure I could, too.

"Are you going to grow horns?"

"Shut up."

"Just checking. You should settle on a boyfriend in case you need someone to milk you."

"Chloe, will you knock it off?"

She looked at me, serious. "I read about it on line. You've got a couple of weeks before your milk comes in. Whoever did this to you was kinky as fuck. It was supposed to be a way for mothers who couldn't nurse to get their hands on breast milk, but the guy who did it used cow udders. They wanted big boobs that made lots of milk, and they got udders."

I didn't know how to ask, but it was desperately important. "Chloe, will I have cow's milk?"

She grinned, holding a pointed wedge of pizza to her lips. "No, you were right. I checked. Girl milk, but *lots*. The thing with tits is that they're about half milk when they're full. You're going to make it by the gallon. Lots of gallons."

"Oh." I cupped the front of my breasts. My nipples stuck out between my fingers, madly erect.

"I can see your heart beating."

"Chloe!" I could feel it too. My breasts felt good. I could never let anyone know that. I couldn't let anyone see me like this.

"When your milk comes in they'll fill up until they're just bags of milk." She paused. "I'm talking four or five times this big, baby girl."

My slice was gone. I picked up another one and bit off half of it. "Not really."

"I've seen pictures. They were big before they got milk, but nothing like you. You're enormous. You won't be able to move. There, I've said it. There's not a chance you'll be able to stand up when they're full. You need to get ready now."

I said, plaintively, "How?"

"You're moving in here. I'm having the pool cleaned out and filled, and when you're really huge you can let the water support them. They probably won't be able to take their own weight. Also it'll give you something to drink."

"Why?"

"You'll need easily five gallons a day. You can't get that from a cup."

I choked on my pizza, swallowed it half-chewed, and washed it down with milk. "What?!" I'd pictured a mason jar brimming with milk, maybe two of them, one from each breast. This was too much, but my nipples felt like rockets about to blast off. I wanted to put my face in my hands, but I was greasy with pizza and my breasts were in the way, too big and too close.

We talked, and I tried to tell Chloe this couldn't be real. She was adamant, and she made more sense than I liked. Eventually she told me to go home, and we'd see each other in the morning.

She loaned me an old baggy jacket and I pulled it closed, squashing enormous breasts that I still couldn't accept were going to be part of me from now on, and I walked home, clutching them inside the rough fabric. I went straight to bed.

I slept badly, unable to turn over without waking up and holding my tits.

At four I got up and walked to the bathroom, top-heavy and unstable. I didn't turn on the light. My breasts stuck out enormously in front of me and I hit the right one on the door to my room, but its immense firm softness cushioned the impact and it didn't hurt. I felt my way down the hall, twice nudging the wall with breasts wider than my shoulders. My massively swollen nipples found the doorframe and I stepped inside the room.

I reached the for the light switch, decided not to bother, and sat on the toilet in the dark, breasts resting on my thighs. It was hard to stand up, but I made it, and I found the sink, easily. My nipples crushed into the taps when I leaned over, and I could feel the outline of the handles with them. I had to lean up to turn them on, and I washed my hands by touch, warm water splashing the underside of my breasts. I knew where the towel rail was, and my breasts found it first, the thick fabric rough and luxurious against their sensitive skin. I dried my hands and blindly stuffed the towel back over the rail.

I went back to my room in the dark, but I misjudged the width of the corridor and my breasts bumped silently into the wall. I turned in the proper direction and walked ahead, relying on them to stop me if I walked into something else. Air currents washed gently over their surfaces and I could almost feel the shape of the room in its subtle movement. It felt cool and erotic.

I stumbled over my bed and got back under the covers, then lay in the dark, unable to sleep, afraid to turn on the light because I knew my breasts were enormously bigger than before. After a while my thoughts became disjointed and the world faded away.

It was light, and Chloe was knocking at my window. I sat up, rocking on my ass like a child's toy, a plastic cartoon creature with breasts bigger than she was, fell back, tried again, twice, and made it to my feet. I stood for a few seconds getting my balance, impossibly top-heavy.

Chloe lifted the window from the outside. "That was amazing. You're so deliciously clumsy. Like you're trapped by your boobs."

I leaned forwards, stubbed my breasts into the window, turned sideways and propped it open with a stick. "I *am*. It's not amazing from here. They're just impossible." My nipples throbbed and I scratched them. My breasts wobbled under my fingers.

"You won't be able to reach those in a few days."

I snorted. "They won't get that big. Idiot."

She shook her head. "You have to move in with me. Today."

"Chloe, I can't. This isn't real. They can't stay like this."

She relented. "Just in case, okay?"

We moved that afternoon. All our friends came and helped.

I was useless. I ate, and I wore a ridiculously huge shirt that was tight across my enormous bust, so people could see how enormous I was. That kept everyone working.

I couldn't lift anything that took both hands, or move it any distance. They made sure I was fed and asked what I wanted to do with stuff. I gave most of it away. When I tried to help they took things out of my hands and moved me to one side, friendly and concerned, as though I'd contracted a strange disease and needed to be taken care of. I supposed I had. I ate all afternoon and drank what felt like gallons of water and energy drinks, and I rode back and forth to thrift shops and bookstores in their trucks. After a few trips the bounce and sway of my breasts felt normal. One of the guys ran a red light and narrowly missed another car. He'd been watching my breasts bounce instead of the road. After that they only let women drive. That helped a bit, but they watched me, too.

Chloe said, "That's a good sign. Everyone still thinks you're sexy."

I didn't feel sexy. I was enormous and clumsy. When they'd moved everything I walked through the empty apartment, looking for stuff we'd missed, but I couldn't see the floor over my breasts, except in the far corner of each room. The kitchen sink wasn't clean, but when I got close it vanished beneath my outthrust chest. I couldn't turn the taps on with my breasts squashed against them, or reach into the bowl. I gave up and left.

An hour later we unpacked the few things I'd kept into Chloe's spare bedroom, and I was home.

I ordered pizza for everyone who'd helped, and we sat around and ate and drank beer. Everyone took care of me, again, and I felt like some kind of strange pet. I ate, feeling bottomless, and drank most of a case of beer by myself. I didn't feel drunk, but I went to bed early, exhausted.

The next morning it took me four tries to sit up. A cow's udder is probably a tenth of its body weight, hung neatly between its four legs. Cows are huge and they don't move fast. When I looked in the mirror I was still little and skinny, and a rack of breasts bigger than I was stuck hugely out in front of me.

Chloe came in to check on me. "Are you okay? Holy shit! You're fucking kidding! They're impossible."

"Thanks."

"Come into the kitchen and I'll make breakfast. You look hungry."

I sat at her counter and rested my breasts on a folded bath towel. The fuzzy surface felt good.

She said, "Feeling okay?"

"Chloe, let's go and do something! I'm feeling cooped up."

"You can't. Look at the size of those things. You should be in the pool."

That worried me. "I'm not some exotic pet you've bought. I can't never do anything. I want to go out."

She smiled. "Sorry. Have a shower and we'll find you some clothes and go out for lunch."

"Okay. Thanks." Chloe was my friend, I'd known her forever, and I trusted her, but she's always been the one who takes care of me and organizes things. I get into trouble and make fun stuff happen. For her this was more of the same. I wasn't really a pet but I hadn't been exactly wrong.

I lifted my breasts off the counter and draped the towel over them so I wouldn't be completely naked.

Chloe said, "That makes them look even bigger."

"Piss off." I walked carefully to the bathroom, feeling heavy and awkward, and bent over to turn on the shower. Chloe's shower is the kind you turn all the way on and wait for the water to get hot. I rotated the handle to the left and stepped back out of the way. Freezing cold water sprayed from the nozzle just as my back hit the glass wall, but my breasts stuck out into the stream of freezing water. I twisted sideways and couldn't get away from under it.

Chloe opened the door and reached through the hundred tiny jets to turn the control off. "Stop being inept. Go out."

I waited, shivering, while she adjusted the temperature. "Chloe, I'm freezing!"

"Come on in."

She let me have the gloriously hot water until I was warm. Chloe and I have showered together hundreds of times, since we were little. I'm almost sure there's nothing more to it than getting clean.

She said, "Can you wash those things?"

"Are you offering?"

"I'm not going to run out of hot water while you fumble around. I know what you're like. You'll be in here all day." She washed herself, quickly and efficiently, shampooed her hair and put conditioner on it. Chloe isn't that tall, though she's got several inches on me, and she has a nice figure, with a small waist and wide hips. Before now I'd thought she had big breasts.

She soaped a sponge and did my back. I said, "Chloe, you've got nice boobs."

"Hush. Nobody's ever going to look at them with you around."

That was completely untrue. Chloe never has a steady boyfriend, but every few days she picks one from her collection and takes him home. I can always tell when it's coming because she wears a tight shirt with her cleavage showing, and she looks good.

She did my breasts next, soaping a hand and working it all over them while I stood with my back to the hot water. "Stop being useless." She put the soap in my hand. "Do your face."

I did, dreamily, while she rubbed soap into my nipples. They swelled into blunt cones.

"This isn't sexy. Pay attention."

"It's not deliberate, Chloe. It's just nice."

"Well, they do look nice."

I tried to see. I wailed, "Chloe, I can't see them!"

"Oh. Sorry. It's not a big deal." She stuck both hands between them and washed me, then did underneath them, and down to my crotch. "Spread your legs."

"Really?"

"Do you want this to take all day? Fuck, I'd rather be in here with some well-hung guy, not washing my friend who got herself into a stupid jam."

Chloe's love for big cocks is well known. I said, "I'd like to be in here with someone cute and intelligent."

"You are." She soaped areas of me that I didn't think anyone else would wash, efficient and thorough. "A guy would watch you being useless and try to fuck you."

"Well, if he was in the shower that would be a reasonable thing to want." I sighed. "This is actually pretty nice."

"Hush." She did my thighs and calves. "Pick up your foot." She did each one, crouching, while I held onto her shoulder. I could just see her between my breasts.

She stood up. "Okay, rinse off."

"Chloe ..."

"For fuck's sake!" She unclipped the showerhead and rinsed me, using her fingers to sluice away the film of soap. "Move your tits so I can get between them."

I pulled them apart with my hands, self-conscious. She sprayed under them, did my back, crotch, and legs. It felt good.

"Ready to get out?"

I said, dreamily, "I'd like to stay in a bit longer."

"We're going out. I'm not having you make yourself come and then go to sleep."

"Chloe, that was really nice."

"You're not using me for sex. Call a boy and send him a picture of your tits."

"I can absolutely not do that. This is bad enough."
She shut off the water. "Then dry yourself and let's go."
I wailed, "I don't know *how*."
"Why are you so useless?!" She wrapped me in a towel, quickly dried herself and put her hair up, and then rubbed me down, being rough everywhere except my breasts, which were too soft and squashed out of the way.

I knew I'd pushed my luck far enough, so I picked out pants and shoes and found, amazingly, a dark green top I could squeeze into.

Chloe came in, perfectly dressed, and tossed a bag at me. "Here. From Aunt Stevie. She got it by mail, and it's way too big for her. But listen, this is it. There aren't any more. If you get bigger you're on your own."

I leaned over and put it on, and did the straps up. It was snug and perfect. I reached into the cups and made sure my nipples were neatly flattened, but the cold air had made them smaller. I pulled the top on. "Tell her I love her."

"Good. Let's go."

We took a bus down to the mall and I stood, clutching a metal pole and feeling my breasts jiggle inside my bra with each bump and turn. We walked the length of the mall, which went on forever, and I started to feel more comfortable moving around, despite being vastly too top-heavy. I was getting used to not seeing the floor ten feet in front of me.

Chloe tried on a dozen outfits. There was nothing that would fit me, except pants, and I wasn't in the mood. I stopped and gazed in the window of a lingerie shop, entranced by a display of bras with enormous lacy cups. Chloe said, "Want to go in?"

"No. I'm short of cash, and this one still fits."

"Come on, ninny. At least try."

We spent a glorious hour being fitted and trying them on, and when I went to leave Chloe pulled out a card and said, "We'll take the red one. The big one."

The salesgirl, a plump creature with breasts not that much smaller than mine, nodded and ran it through. She said, "I'll give you twenty percent off. I imagine they'll still grow."

I stared at her, wide eyed.

She said, "I got caught too. But you're bigger."

The food court was harsh and public. Chloe knew a bar on the garden level and we sat at a table under a dozen huge ferns. I rested my breasts on the table and took my new bra out to admire it.

The waitress came up. She wasn't that old, and she had a staggering hourglass figure, wide hips and a wasp waist, with huge breasts that nearly overflowed her skintight red dress. If I hadn't been there she'd have been enormous.

She said, "Hi. You've had the treatment. Are you really going to go for it?"

Chloe sad, "Huh?"

She knelt down and spoke more quietly. "I got stung at a party, and by the time my parents got me the cure I was like this." She giggled. "I love my boobs, but I can't get a serious job. People just stare into my cleavage."

I said, "There's a cure?!"

"Yeah, you can get it online. It doesn't make them go away." She adjusted her left breast. "I guess I couldn't go back anyway. Do you know that if you wait long enough you get milk? That's freaky." She raised her pad. "I'll put you down for a big steak and a beer." She looked at Chloe. "Monte Cristo and a diet coke?"

"Sure."

When she was gone I said, "Chloe. I have to find this cure, before it's too late."

"As soon as we get home. Can we eat lunch?"

"Yes. Crap, this changes everything." I wanted to say that I could have a life again, but I was afraid it was too late. "How long does it take to work? What if I get milk first?"

"It's okay." She patted my arm. "Can we eat first?"

The waitress brought me a huge mug of draft beer, and a steak that covered most of the plate. "That's because you're one of us."

I said, "How did you get this?"

She smiled. "Lesson one: when you're built like this you can get anything. The chef can't look at me and say no." She looked at my breasts, easily twice the size of hers. "You must know that."

I'd been too busy trying to adapt to not being skinny and flat that I hadn't tried. It had seemed like cheating. Why had I run from that car? I could have demanded a ride home. "I guess so." I devoured my steak and washed it down with beer. When the mug was empty she brought me another. I ate everything on my plate, famished, and two slices of cheesecake.

When we were ready to leave the waitress said, "I lost your bill."
She hugged me, massive breasts pressing into mine. "You're cool.
Let me know how it goes."

I realized I was drunk, and I walked unevenly down the mall,
barely managing to keep myself upright. My breasts felt enormously
heavy. I said, "Chloe, I think I should lie down."

"I think so. You're not up to a bus."

I said, slurring my words slightly, "I don't need a bus, I have
boobs." We'd reached the main doors. I led her outside, clinging to
her arm for support, and found a young man getting into a truck. I
walked up to him and stuck my chest out, trying to aim my breasts
straight at him. "Hello. My friend and need a ride. It's only twenty
blocks."

He goggled at me. "Get in."

I managed to do my seat belt up around my bust, and Chloe gave
him instructions. Fifteen minutes later he pulled up in front of her
house. "If you two ever need a ride again, just call." He gave Chloe
a card.

Chloe dragged me into the house and I lay on the couch, clutching
the bag with my new bra. Pretty soon I slept.

When woke up it was dark. I was wearing my panties and socks,
and had a blanket over me. Something loomed up between my face
and the dim light from the kitchen. It was my breasts, grown even
more gigantic. I struggled halfway upright, heavy and clumsy. I
knew, blurrily, that they couldn't weigh more than my hips and legs,
but they held me down. I managed to roll over onto the floor on
hands and knees, and they hung like udders, round and massively
heavy, pressing sideways into my arms.

I was terrified that Chloe would come and see me like this. I
grabbed the corner of the bed, desperate, and pulled upright. I made
it to my feet, but I was impossibly awkward. Half the room seemed
to be full of the upward swell of my naked bust. My arms extended
out to my sides, steadying me, and I took a small, careful step, and
another. My breasts tried to pull me over forward, but I got my
balance and was fairly steady.

I walked gingerly into the kitchen and leaned down so I could see
over my breasts to read the clock on the oven. The red letters made
my skin glow. It was three in the morning.

I was hungry. I'd hoped there would be a bottle of pills on the table
labeled 'antidote,' but there was a nothing but a note from Chloe.
'Might have a line on the antidote. Don't worry.'

A meat pie sat on the counter beside the stove, in a tinfoil dish.
She'd ordered it for me. I was touched, and famished. I ate a slice,
and then another. Half an hour later I'd polished off the whole thing.

I went back to the living room and dressed, got into my black jeans
and managed to pull the top I'd worn before over my even bigger
bust. The fabric was stretched as tight as it would stand, my nipples
crushed flat and perfectly outlined.

I thought for a moment and peeled it off, and I pulled on the bra
Chloe had bought me. It was snug and comfortable, but for the first
time I didn't really feel as though I needed one - it wasn't supporting
my breasts so much as stretched tight over them. They'd gone from
being barely there to round and firm, then big and soft, and huge and
teardrop shaped. I hadn't noticed them pulling up into rounded,
bulging cones like fat artillery shells, but suddenly they were
impossibly firm and rather than hanging gently down they stuck
straight out in front of me. I couldn't be sure, but to my hands it felt
like a foot and a half. I took off the bra, carefully folded it and put it
away, and squeezed into the top again.

I went down to the living room and opened the window onto the
lawn. The front door was much too public, and my huge breasts
made me feel painfully shy. I'd never been like that before.

I'd thought I'd lean over the sill and figure out what to do when my
breasts were outside, but they hit the edge of the frame halfway up.
Confused, I felt under them. Their huge bases occupied the entire
front of my chest. I took a deep breath and they moved and jostled
each other. The bottom half of my field of vision was filled with
two pale pink hemispheres. I couldn't see my nipples.

I realized that I'd had no idea what I'd do when I was dangling out
of the window, off balance. I'd either have fallen out headfirst or,
worse, been stuck.

I walked down to the front door, as silently as I could, although the
floor creaked under my careful feet. My body was the same as it had
always been, but my breasts were immensely heavy. I took half a
dozen deep breaths and turned the handle. The front door opened
into a world where I was insanely busty, a freak, and people would
stare at me. I stepped out, turned ponderously, and closed the door

behind me.

The night was dark and wonderful. I walked through the silent neighborhood, barefoot, wishing I could walk naked, but afraid of how brightly my pale skin would reflect the streetlights.

A car passed me, but I was just a shadowy figure in the dark space between light poles. I hesitated, but I couldn't resist the cool air. I undid the buttons halfway down my top, and then further, past the furthest bulge of my breasts. White cleavage gaped between my lapels, and I felt too visible, but I didn't care. For the first time I understood how gorgeously big my breasts were. I undid more buttons, and my fingertips came to the last one before I expected it. The shirt fell open, loose, and my breasts pulled the lapels apart and stuck out, enormous round peaks. I fumbled for the bottom button. Headlights turned a corner and drove towards me.

I frantically clutched the front together and turned away, trying not be obvious. A streetlight shone down on me and my breasts glowed like huge, pale lamps. I got ready to run, not sure I still could. The car swept past and disappeared.

The back alleys were safe and dark, and I turned down one. I pulled my shirt together and started doing up two buttons, but the night air blew over me, like a drug. I opened them again and let the wind eddy round my breasts. The shirt pulled back, and they stuck out like small soft mountains, pink icebergs. I took a deep breath and put my shoulders back, and the pink globes reared up in front of me. My hands felt the pointed fronts and my big round nipples.

The alley was rough under my feet, but I kept going, and when no cars drove down the dark lane I stripped my shirt completely off and carried it in one hand. My breasts were creamy white in the light from windows and streetlights. I wondered if this wasn't more idiotic than walking on the sidewalk where there were places to escape into and bushes to hide behind.

The alley lit up to one side of me, and a car swept found the corner. Terrified, I ducked backwards into a stack of garbage cans, and knelt on filthy concrete as wheels crunched past on loose gravel. Beams of yellow light caught the tips of my breasts where they stuck out between the bins, but they were twin cones, part of something else, too big to be part of a small and half-naked woman.

The car vanished down the narrow path, and I waited, heaved myself to my feet, and brushed grit off my knees. I kept going,

scanning the alley ahead for hiding places, but no more cars came.
Half a block further on I gave in to an irresistible, dangerous desire.
I shucked out of my pants and walked naked, the night air streaming
over my body, my nipples hard and erect. I was terrifyingly
exposed, and my skin glowed where light from yards and houses
penetrated into the gloomy alley, but I couldn't stop.

An hour later I was a mile from home, lost and still naked. I'd
dropped my clothes somewhere, running desperately across a lawn
and onto a silent, dark porch, trying to escape from the unflinching
gaze of two brilliant headlights, then ducking behind a patch of high
bushes when a light had come on inside. When a door had opened
I'd panicked and run around the house and down two alleys, my
breasts bouncing even more hugely than before, ungainly and
terrifying. When I'd calmed down and stopped gasping for air I'd
been lost, unable to find my way back. I'd wandered for another half
hour, stepping furtively out of the tenuous safety of the shadows to
look at street signs, scared, enormously busty and naked, desperate
to find my way home, certain I was getting further and further away.

I found a street I recognized it and followed it for half a mile,
dashing clumsily through trees and gardens put there to block the
view and the noise of traffic. A dozen cars passed, intent on their
business, not seeing the pale figure immobile in the shadows.

When I was five blocks from home I cut between two dark houses
out onto the street and proudly walked down the sidewalk, naked and
glowing in the street lights.

The door was locked.

I didn't care. I could crawl in through a window. I walked round to
the side and found the one Chloe has used, and lifted up on the
bottom. Nothing happened. It was dark inside, but I could see the
brass catch on the window frame. Chloe had locked me out. I stared
into the glass, unable for a moment to think. A streetlight cast a few
rays down beside the house, and I saw my reflection in the glass, a
slender, naked girl with a mass of black hair and immense firm
breasts, far too big for her skinny body. She looked scared and tired.

I studied her for a minute, staggered but not entirely displeased,
before I came back to myself. My breasts were heavy and the night
air was cooling off. I tried the window again, silently, but it was
firmly locked.

I tiptoed around to the front door, holding my breasts in my hands so they wouldn't sway and throw me off balance, rolling my hips so I could keep my shoulders steady, tired and suddenly awkward. I wondered if the guy with the pills had picked me because I was the girl they'd look the most outsized on.

I rang the bell and pounded on the door, but nothing happened. Chloe wouldn't answer the door when it was dark, and she slept like a rock. I pounded again. A minute later lights turned the corner and shone down the block. I ran back between the houses. The car drove past.

I didn't know what time it was. It would get light in a few hours, maybe a lot less, and I couldn't be seen stark naked with these huge breasts. I felt like a vampire, safe while the world slept, but scared of the approaching dawn.

My place was twenty blocks away, over two miles, but it would still be empty. I'd paid the rent until the end of the month. I kept a key on top of the doorframe.

The sky looked light in the east. I set off, not part of the night any more, just me, naked and alone.

The first ten blocks were easy. I walked among rows of houses. The lawns were well kept, with lots of trees and shrubs, and I walked across lawns, next to the houses, intermittently shielded from the road. A few cars came past and each time I crouched behind a bush or a tree.

I knew I couldn't keep doing that. It was getting late. Lights came on behind windows. A car pulled out of a garage, and then another. I told myself none of these people would be late for work to hunt a naked girl. Probably they'd call the police. Crap!

I moved faster, not quite panicking, but letting my huge breasts wobble and bounce, sometimes dashing for a few steps to get from a bush to the cover of a tree or a porch. Each time a car went by I cursed the waste of time until its awful lights were gone.

I crossed a main road, waiting a precious five minutes while the sky slowly lightened, waiting for the road to be empty, finally chancing a frantic dash across when there was only one car, two blocks away. On the other side was not the houses I'd expected but an empty lot, and I had to walk across rutted mud, exposed and naked. I wanted to sprint over the uneven ground, but I couldn't see it over my breasts, and I couldn't afford to fall over. I couldn't run fast, either. I forced myself to walk and the car zoomed past. I told myself I was just an indistinct figure in the dark, and they hadn't called the police.

I was in an area of low apartments, but there were still lawns and shrubs. People would be getting up to walk to bus stops, but not yet. I repeated that, *not yet*, trying not to panic and run.

A door opened and I stepped between two parked cars and crouched down. A man in a suit stepped out, paused to look at the sky, and turned the other way. I ran, silent on bare feet, bent over, clutching huge breasts that shook in my desperately spread fingers.

I made it another two blocks. This time a woman walked briskly out and right past me, mesmerized by her phone. I stepped into a patch of shade, my breasts sticking out into the light, too big to conceal. Twenty feet further on she opened a car door with a remote, still talking, and got in. I didn't have time to wait for her to drive away. I stepped out and walked past her, nearly running, telling myself I couldn't hurry. She put the car in gear, still on her phone, and pulled away from the curb.

A garbage truck drove by and I crouched down in a patch of shrubs that didn't come above my knees. I tried to curl up but my breasts were too big to let me. They crushed into my thighs and chest and bulged up into my field of view. The guys who drove that thing would chase me down like a trophy. Fuck, they'd be right. I looked down at my tits, pale pink in the first light of day. I was prey, the deer with the biggest rack, grown by the man with the pills and released for this moment. I'd have liked to kill him but I was small and naked, impossibly busty and awkward. If he was here I'd run.

The truck turned a corner, but there were four cars coming. I waited, terrified. When the last one was barely past me I stood up, looked around, and ran. Nobody looks to the side when they're driving a car. I knew that was nonsense, but I was too far from home and the sky was pale blue in the east.

I made it another three blocks before a car drove past. By now there were no trees, so I crouched on the sidewalk by a car, knowing that if anyone came out of a building I was caught. It was a taxi, and that was dangerous because there'd be a passenger. It sped by and vanished. Nobody would ask a taxi to stop so they could look for a naked girl, even a fabulously busty one.

The next time there was a rental sign, and I stood behind it, pressing my breasts into the weathered, rough plywood. When the lights moved past I made myself step out and continue.

On another block was a tiny park. I hid beneath the hanging branches of a huge fir tree, in a small, perfect space, and I thought of staying there until it was dark and quiet again. I couldn't survive a day without food or a place to pee. It was too scary. I kept going.

I walked down a row of shops, old ones with inset doors. I moved more quickly, then forced myself to slow down. You're more noticeable running, though that doesn't make much difference if you're naked. My breasts were comfortable at a walk, bouncy and ridiculous when I ran. A car went past, and I hid in a doorway, slightly less exposed. Brakes screeched and someone honked and yelled. Fuck, the driver had seen me.

I peeked out and the man in the truck behind him had got out, yelling. I stepped out, my heart pounding, and walked away. They were too concerned with their fight to see me, even though it was my fault. I was too panicked to care.

At the corner I turned and walked fast to the end of the block, not quite running. That took me further from the safety of home, but there were no cars right then. I had to keep moving. I turned right again.

This street was less trafficked, and I relaxed a bit. What would I do if I got home and they'd changed the lock or taken my key? I wondered if I could make a mad dash back to Chloe's place and hide between the houses, but there was no way. Why hadn't I stayed there? There was no cover, but by now I didn't care. It was too late. I was exhausted and I could dash for twenty feet, maybe less. I was hungry and thirsty, and I needed to lie down and sleep.

I made it three blocks. Half a dozen cars passed, but there were trucks parked along the side of the road and I stayed beside them, dashing across brief gaps when the road was empty. Perils that would have had me crouching, terrified, a mere hour ago, were now acceptable risks.

A man came out of a shop and I ducked between two huge delivery trucks. They were parked so close together that I had to squeeze in. My butt touched one and my breasts squashed against the other, picking up a layer of grey dust. I held my breath and heard a truck start with a clatter of valves, a diesel. Maybe if I stepped out he'd give me a ride home. I didn't dare, so I stood, naked and dirty, as he pulled out. Red and amber taillights lit up my almost useless hiding space and he was gone.

I slid out and brushed myself with my hands, dismayed that I'd allowed my huge, perfect breasts to get covered in grime. Most of it didn't come off, and my hands left dirty smears across my nipples. Less than a minute later another truck started. I hadn't seen the driver. I ducked between two cars and crouched, looking back at him through a windshield and a back window. The sheet metal was almost painfully cold where my breasts pressed into it. I stood on my toes and steadied myself with my hands, my body vibrating, tense. The sidewalk was empty, so I stood and walked to the corner, twenty feet away, and turned onto the side street.

The sky was light now, and as I walked past a store fluorescents came on behind big glass windows, surrounding me with light. I said, "Shit," and ran four paces past it, not caring how much I bounced. Another one lit up before I got there, and I dashed past, clutching my breasts to my chest, terrified, almost in tears.

The next block was still dark, but there were only a handful of cars for cover. I walked down it, quickly, crouching once behind a filthy SUV as two trucks drove past. Ten seconds later I hid between an empty planter and a concrete wall. Headlights hit my breasts, making them glow creamy white, but the rest of me was in shadow. I was making almost no progress.

I ducked into the alley to catch my breath, my heart pounding again, and I wondered if I could hide all day between dumpster and empty cardboard boxes. I knew I couldn't, and I was wasting moments I couldn't spare at all. I forced myself to go back out. As I turned the corner lights came on at the far end, illuminating me from behind, and the giant shadow of a naked girl shone on the concrete wall across the street, washed out by the dawn. I was out of time.

Fuck. I wondered if I could make it back to my tree. I stood between two trucks, ready to give up, as five more went by. The one ahead of me had a topper on it, and I thought about crawling in and going to sleep, but the big side windows were clean and there was no trash to hide in.

I stepped out and continued. The convenience store on the corner had its lights on, but it always had. I'd shopped there at odd hours, a hundred times. I was a block from home.

I ran, desperate, crouched over, hips wobbling, holding my breasts in my hands to steady them. A man walked down the sidewalk and I ducked between two cars, no longer hesitating. He passed me, not looking to the side. I was filthy from crouching between vehicles covered in dust and dirt. I didn't care. I walked past a woman struggling to open a door with a sidewalk sign in her hands, and behind a man crouched over, filling a red metal dispenser with flyers.

Someone yelled, "Hey!"

I was at the door to my building. I opened it and stepped inside.

The lobby was small and gloomy, and there was no outside door lock. The elevator dinged, and a second later it started to rumble open. I stepped to the stairwell door and pushed it open, more with my breasts than my hands, stepped through, and let it close.

I lived on the sixth floor. I took the first three flights of stairs quickly, my breasts bouncing up and down in time, scared because if you lived on the lower floors it would be easier to take the stairs down and not wait for an elevator. I slowed down on the fourth flight. When I was ten feet from the top the door I'd just passed opened. A man stepped out and lit a cigarette. I tiptoed up the last few steps, silently, breathing heavily through my open mouth.

At the top I turned to the fifth flight. I'd done this before, but not carrying these enormous, heavy breasts, and my legs were burning. I trudged up another half flight and paused for my thighs and calves to recover, trying to catch my breath. I stopped again at the top.

The last flight was agony. I climbed two steps, stopped, managed two more, and paused again. A door opened far below me and slammed, and the sound echoed up the concrete walls. Footsteps headed down, fading. I wondered, still a night creature, how it didn't scare people in shoes to make so much noise.

I took the last dozen steps one at a time, my throat raw, pulling myself up with the railing. The door at the top had a tiny glass window and I looked through it, sure the people in nearby apartments could hear me gasping for air. A door opened and a man came out, shut it, and waited for an elevator. I watched in agony, desperate to be safe, to pee, and to sleep, even if only on a carpeted floor. When the elevator doors closed another man came out, and a woman, and four more people. I waited, my great dusty breasts pressed into the brown metal door, starting to shiver. I didn't know what to do.

People got on the elevator and left, and I pulled back. There were two big circles of dust on the door. I wiped them off, even though nobody would ever notice or connect them to me.

A woman came out of an apartment, wearing a long black coat, a neighbor I vaguely recognized. She glanced at my door and I pulled back. The elevator dinged and she got on.

I waited, desperate, and counted to twenty, not sure why, before I opened the door and ran the ten steps to my apartment, more naked than ever. My huge breasts squashed massively into the door.

I reached up to the top of the frame, and my fingers found nothing. I sobbed, out loud, once, slid them along to the right, and I had it. I fumbled it into the lock as I heard another doorhandle turn, twisted it, pushed, and fell inside. I let it shut behind me. I was safe.

I'd forgotten about my couch. It had been supposed to go to the thrift store, but someone had left it here. I walked to the bathroom, peed for a long time, then went back to the couch, laid down, and closed my eyes. The room was warm and quiet, and ten seconds later I was asleep.

I could smell food cooking, and someone said, "You're awake?" There was a blanket over me.

I sat up, pulling the blanket over my chest. "Hi. Who are you?"

"I live here. I'm Linda. Who are you?"

"This is my place until the end of the month."

She smiled. "The landlord said you'd gone, and he was sure you wouldn't mind if I moved in early. It's better than sitting in a hotel. But what are you doing here, naked?"

I made sure the blanket covered my breasts. "It's a long story. I got locked out of my new place, so I came here."

She said, "You took a pill from someone you didn't know. Here, you'll be famished. I've made food." She scooped a dozen fried eggs onto a huge plate, added half a dozen sausages and a huge pile of hash browns, and put it in front of me with a glass of milk that held at least a quart.

I said, "Thanks. I can't eat all of this."

"Hang on. Fried tomatoes." She dropped five wedges off a spatula onto a small empty space. It looked delightful. I picked up my fork.

I ate a quarter of it before I stopped to drink my milk. When I looked again it was more than half gone. I didn't care.

She said, "So you took the pill, or did someone put it in your drink?"

I said, between huge mouthfuls, "I took it. It was stupid."

"You're not alone. But why haven't you taken the antidote? Your boobs are nice, but they're pretty huge."

"Chloe, my friend. She's getting it, but it's hard to find."

She paused for two seconds, considering her words. "No, it's not. Are you lovers? Did she give you the pill?"

"No, she's just my friend. She's taking care of me."

She said, "How long have you known her?"

"Forever."

"Hm. Listen, a lot of people got the pills from a friend. Sometimes it's revenge, feelings of inferiority, or just because they want the friend to have big boobs. If you have the antidote you can let your friend get really big and then give it to them."

"Why would they do that?"

"Because they were afraid to do it to themself? I don't know. But the antidote is easy to get."

"Chloe will get it." I went back to eating.

Linda said, slowly, "There's what we call 'exotic pet syndrome.' It's when someone loves someone and wants to take care of them. If their breasts are too big they'll always need help."

I said, "Okay, but Chloe's always been the sensible one. I have fun and she makes sure nobody gets hurt." I was beginning to feel full, but the food was very good. I drank some more milk.

She said, "So why hasn't she given you the antidote? She has it."

"She doesn't."

She said, "Is it fun having big tits?"

"No, but I'm getting used to it."

"So instead of being fun, you're quiet, and Chloe takes care of you."

"No, it's not like that." I ate the last egg in two bites. "Thank you. I'm stuffed, and that was wonderful. Can I stay until it gets dark?"

"Sure. It's really your place. Why?"

"I can't walk home in daylight. I'm naked."

"Oh. I might have some clothes that will fit you."

I sighed. "I doubt it."

"Then I'll give you a ride."

"Now?" I was feeling tired, and I wanted a nap. "Can we do it later?"

"Sure. Want my bed?"

"The couch is fine."

She nodded. "Sleep, and I'll make lunch."

"I'm never eating again."

"Until you have the antidote you'll need lots of food. At least you didn't drink the whole gallon of milk."

"Why?"

"Once you start being really thirsty you're only a couple of days away from having milk, and then it's too late. I'm assuming you're a milker."

"I think so. Chloe says I am."

"How does she know?"

I shrugged. "She knows stuff like that."

She sounded resigned. "Okay."

I said, "Too late for what?"

"To stop. If you get the antidote you'll still have the boobs but you'll stop getting bigger."

"How do you know?" I was too sleepy to concentrate.

She said, "I've researched this. My friend's daughter has them. Not as big as yours, but that's what got me into this. She was terrified." She sighed. "You're almost all little and skinny, and you can't resist big breasts. It's like you're the basic girl you can add huge boobs to."

I yawned. "Huh. But the antidote doesn't fix them."

"No. It stops them getting bigger." She sounded frustrated. "You're the biggest I've seen. You have to get the antidote right away."

"Chloe will get it for me." I couldn't admit that might not be true.

I slept until after noon. Linda woke me with a plate of food, and I ate it all, and I politely asked for more, which she made. My breasts felt heavier but I didn't mind.

She said, "You should phone your friend."

"Oh. My phone is at home."

She held one out. "Do you know the number?"

"Yes." I dialed, and Chloe answered after the first two rings. "Hello?"

"Hi. It's me. I went for a walk and lost my clothes, and I couldn't get in."

She said, "I've been worried sick. I'll come and get you."

"No, Linda says she'll bring me back later. Did you get the antidote?"

"It's pretty hard to get, but I have a line on it. Probably tomorrow."

"Okay. I'll see you in a couple of hours."

"All right. Be careful."

"Bye." I hung up.

Linda led me to a bed and put me in it. My breasts stuck up under the thick blankets like a diorama of mountains. When she left I tried to roll onto my front, but that was impossible. I got on all fours and lowered myself onto them, but they didn't squash the way they once had. When I lay on my side it was as bad. I rolled onto my back and was comfortable, but I was half uncovered. "Linda!"

She came in. "You can't sleep?"

"I can't get the covers to work."

She pulled them back into place. "All the girls like you have problems. I'm going to get you the antidote."

"No, it's fine." I shut my eyes.

She tiptoed out and shut the door.

When I woke it was dusk. I went out and found Linda putting away groceries. "Hi. Sit here." She pointed to a tall chair. "I'll make you some supper."

I said, "You like to care for people, too."

"You seem to need it." She poured a glass of milk. "Let me finish this cupboard. Are those things larger?"

I didn't have to lean down to rest them on the counter. Maybe the stool wasn't very high. They bulged upwards more, and stuck out further from my chest. "I don't know. Probably." I was so used to them getting bigger that I didn't know.

She made spaghetti and gave me a plate with a huge amount of thick meat sauce. "If you're going to eat something messy, it might as well be when you're naked."

I had four plates, and by the end I was greasy down as far as I could see, over the curve of my bust.

Linda said, "Go and have a shower and we'll find you some clothes."

I paused. "Linda, Chloe kind of ... helps me shower."

"Oh. I can't do that." She sighed. "I'm sorry."

I didn't know if I could wash myself. I said, lost, "I can do the dishes." Maybe I could get clean that way.

She looked skeptical, but she let me try. It took me five minutes to wash a plate I couldn't see beneath my bust, and it left my breasts and the floor coated in soapy water. Linda sat me back down and gave me a bowl of ice cream, and I ate it while she finished.

She said, "I'll start the water and set out a couple of big towels."

"Could I have some more ice cream?"

She gave me another bowl, and I savored it. When I was done I said, "Okay, I'm ready. I can do this myself."

"Come on."

Embarrassed, I walked to the shower, naked. I was sure my breasts were heavier than they'd been last night, when being naked and scared had given me energy I didn't have now.

Linda set towels and soap and shampoo out, and hung a housecoat she got from a cardboard box on the back of the doorframe. She turned on the water and adjusted the temperature. "There. That's pretty good. Listen, the bigger you get the more you'll need someone to take care of you."

"I should get the antidote. I know."

"No. Will Chloe take care of you if you stop? Because if you get any bigger you'll have to have her." She sighed. "You do already. You know that."

"I might have to get big enough to make her happy?"

"No. There are programs. You have to stop as soon as you can. But having a friend is better than paying someone." She stepped out of the way and opened the shower door. "I'm saying don't fall out with her if you can avoid it."

"She's my friend. It's okay."

She nodded and left. I maneuvered inside and sat down on the tiled floor. It would be hard to get up, but I was very top-heavy and the floor was slick and invisible, a long way down.

I put shampoo on my hair and soaped my upper body and as much of my legs as I could reach. I wanted to make myself come, but I was afraid the crash after that would leave me more tired and sad than I could handle. Linda was nice, but she wasn't Chloe.

I struggled upright, hanging onto the taps, my breasts sticking out in front of me, and rather than step back and lose my grip I slid them up the tiled wall, happy that Linda couldn't see me. That felt steadier so I leaned into them while I did my butt and thighs. Then I turned around and leaned back, supporting myself on the wall, and did my face. I soaped my breasts, taking my time and doing them carefully.

Chloe would do this better. I wondered if she'd found the antidote yet.

I stood again and rinsed myself. It was hard to get between my breasts, and I couldn't rinse the soap out of my crotch - the water cascaded off my breasts and left me dry down to my thighs. I tried splashing myself, but that didn't work. I was on the verge of asking Linda for a cup to catch water in when I realized the showerhead came off on its hose.

I rinsed myself again, more thoroughly, and then gave in and found the pulse setting. Five minutes later I came, dreamily, sitting on the shower floor and gasping as pleasure burst inside me. I wanted to go to sleep right there, but the hot water was running out. I climbed heavily to my feet, butting the glass with both breasts as I stood up, turned off the water and dried myself, feeling warm and sleepy.

Linda said, "Are you awake?"

"Just barely." I struggled into the housecoat she'd left, and cinched it around my waist. The front didn't close and my breasts stuck out, huge and round. I'd known they would. I didn't care.

Linda was sitting on the couch with a mug of hot chocolate. She pointed to another larger one, for me. I sat down and picked it up. "Thank you."

She said, "Chloe phoned."

"And?" I wanted to be back where someone would take care of me properly.

"She hasn't found the antidote yet. She's going out to talk to some people, and she asked if you could stay here."

"Can I?"

"Since it's your place, of course. You could anyway. But there's another thing."

I said, "She should have got the antidote."

"Yes. I think she's going out so you can't come home, and that puts off your taking it for another day."

"So?"

"I can get it."

"I'll wait."

"Do you know how big you are? You're beyond enormous. Your nipples are bigger across than my boobs."

I said, "I don't mind."

She pulled a cloth tape measure out of her pocket. "Can I measure you?"

"Go ahead." I wanted to say no, but I wasn't sure I could stop her.
She was taller than me.

She wrapped the tape around my right breast, and measured from
my collarbone down to my nipple. "Okay, they're basically fat
cones, but as a rough estimate they're about a foot sphere. More than
a foot. That's each." She picked up her phone and punched numbers
into it. Your breasts weigh about thirty pounds each."

"So? I know they're big."

"The literature says that by this time you're getting about an inch
bigger a day. In four days you'll be sixteen inches each. That's more
than seventy five pounds each. You physically will not be able to
stand up."

I said, "Four days is a long time."

"How much do you weigh? Before you got tits? A hundred
pounds?"

I said, defensively, "A hundred and two. And I'm in good shape."

She snarled, "Your cute little body isn't handling the strain that
well. You're carrying sixty extra pounds on a body that's built to
carry a hundred."

I didn't admit to anything. I thought of running up stairs,
breathless, but that wasn't surprising. I knew she was right.

"I want to get you checked out, okay?"

"Where?"

"I have friends at the university. We can go right now."

"Okay." I'd pushed my luck far enough. Even if I didn't take the
antidote, I needed to know what was happening to me.

"I'll find you some clothes."

Her pants were too big and loose, but she knelt and rolled up the
cuffs while I stood, helpless. She found a belt to hold them up.
None of her tops would fit me at all, so she wrapped a black scarf
round my breasts, safety pinned it at the back, and helped me put on
a small leather jacket over it. "There. You look sexy."

We rode to the university in her car. She helped me in and put my
seatbelt on, but the ride over was okay. The tops of my breasts
rippled as vibrations from the road came up through the suspension,
and they swayed as she turned corners, but she drove carefully and
we made it.

I tried to get out by myself, but the seat was low and I couldn't

quite stand up. She held out a strong hand and pulled me out and to
my feet. An elevator took us to the fifth floor of a concrete building,
and a young woman in a lab coat met us at the door. "Linda! Is this
your protégé?"

"Stacy. No, this is a young idiot I've picked up." She sighed.
"Deb, Stacy. Deb needs the antidote for her breasts, and her owner
won't produce it. I need to know how her body's handling this."

Stacy said, "I'd say she's okay, from looking at her. You know she
can't have more than a few days?"

Linda nodded. "I know. She's bigger than any of my other cases.
She's stubborn."

I said, angrily, "Chloe's working on it. It's okay."

Stacy got a young man, Rob, out of another lab, and they took my
pulse, checked my blood oxygen, made me walk on a treadmill, and
took pictures of my body with a small handheld device I couldn't
identify. Stacy offered me a glass of sugar water and I drank most of
it, and she took a sample of my blood.

An hour and a half later she opened a bag of cookies and we sat
round a table. Rob couldn't tear his eyes away from my breasts. I'd
ditched the jacket when I was on the treadmill, and I realized that the
scarf didn't cover much. I covered my embarrassment by eating
almost all the cookies.

Stacy said, "It's better than I expected. You're running a bit hot, but
you're handling it. You're burning a lot of food, and your
metabolism is up."

"I am not."

She looked at the empty bag. "That was another test. You just ate
a whole bag of cookies. There's another one under the counter if you
want."

I knelt, clumsily, and got them, and pulled myself up on the
counter. It wasn't easy, and my breasts were enormously in the way,
but I did it.

"Okay, you're not immobile yet." Stacy leafed through sheets of
paper. "I expected your heart to be racing, but it's not much faster
than normal. You're breathing okay. You have a pretty big chest
and lungs, but we can't measure directly because your ribcage is half
submerged in breast tissue. Have you always been big there?"

"No. I'm pretty skinny." I shrugged, eating another cookie.

"Again, your metabolism is up, but your liver is handling it. Your digestive tract is okay, kidneys are producing a lot of nitrates but they're not showing any distress. We scanned your lower back, but you're quite muscular there." She turned to Linda. "She's very good in most respects. I think we should consider whether this version modifies other systems."

I said, "So I can handle it?"

She shook her head. "No. You absolutely can't. You're okay now, but your body won't be able to handle the metabolic demands of making the amount of milk you'll have. Not indefinitely. It's little, skinny girls who are attracted to this, when it should be the big, cow-like ones they get." She sighed. "I suppose it wouldn't matter, but it might help a bit. A cow weighs ten times what you do. Your body isn't up to this. You might be able to eat enough to make milk, for a while, but given time you'll slowly starve. You'll need to drink twenty gallons of water a day, and I can't imagine what that'll do to your electrolyte balance. You'll be completely immobile when your breasts are full, and that'll be most of the time." She added, "We'll get you a milking machine, but I don't know how long it'll take to empty you. You have big nipples but they're not cow teats. Until you're lactating we won't know how much milk you can force through them."

I said, "Other girls have done it. You said I'm better adapted."

Linda said, "Most of them got the antidote. Only a handful are milking, and none of them can stand up. They're all slowly starving to death, and they have IVs because they can't force themselves to drink enough. The one who's doing best was clinically obese, and now she's emaciated, except for her tits." She added, "You're already bigger than any of them. It's not something you can survive in the long term. You're not milking yet, but you don't have much time."

I said, "I know. How long has she been like this? Growing?"

"A month and a half, we think. She didn't tell anyone until it was too late. A friend got her to a hospital and they managed to get enough fluids into her with IVs. She's been lactating for just over a month. You can meet her if you want."

I said, "The girl who took her to the hospital. Her owner?"

"Yes."

"Chloe's not my owner."

"It's just a term we use. Most of the girls have a friend who takes care of them. In most cases we're sure the owner gave them the pill."

"Mine was a guy."

Stacy took an envelope out of her pocket. "This is the antidote. It's not an insult to your friend if you take it."

"Linda says Chloe may not take care of me."

"There's an excellent program at the hospital. They'll provide care and training. If you stop before you get bigger, and before you're milking, we expect that you can mostly live by yourself."

I didn't want to live by myself. I wanted to be skinny again. I wanted Chloe. I imagined my breasts sticking two inches further out, then four, and five. "I'll wait. You said I'm in no danger yet."

Linda looked at Stacy.

Stacy said, "I didn't say that. You're like an engine that's running too fast, but it hasn't quit. It's not safe. You're growing very fast. Even if you stop right now, the challenges of living with a bust as big as yours aren't trivial."

"Can I meet someone bigger than me?"

"There *isn't* anyone. Once you start lactating they don't get bigger, except when they're full of milk and they're enormous. Most girls have milk long before they're as big as you."

Linda said, "We're sure she's not?"

"We've offered her drinks three times, and she hasn't finished one."

I said, "So I'm okay."

"*No.*" Stacy looked frustrated and angry. "Having breasts this big means the shock to your system will be even worse when you have milk. I seriously recommend that you take the antidote now."

I said, "I'll wait."

Stacy picked up the envelope and met Linda's eyes. Linda shook her head. Stacy had offered to force the pill down my throat.

I said, "I'll get a lawyer. I'll leave. I can fight you."

Stacy put it down. "You might have until the day after tomorrow. Linda says you're at about twelve inches."

"Yes."

"Two days is fourteen. That's fifty pounds each. You'll be able to stand, but not much else. Another day and you'll be lying on your front, and you'd better hope someone comes to feed you."

I said, "I know. I want to go home and see Chloe."

Linda said, "She's not there. Will you think this over? I'll take you back in the morning, either way."

I nodded. "Yes."

Their eyes met again, and Linda put the envelope in her pocket. Once I was too big to stand up she'd force the pill down my throat. She could hide it in my food. I remembered the taste. I'd know.

I said, "Thank you. This has helped."

Stacy gave me a card. "If you change your mind, no matter when it is, or what time, call me. Okay?"

"Okay."

Linda said, "If Chloe doesn't have anything by tomorrow night, will you agree to take it?"

I shook my head. "I don't know. I'll think about it."

I'd finished both packets of cookies. I got up, immensely top-heavy, my breasts solid and firm, and tried not to look as unsteady as I felt.

Stacy walked with us to the elevator. "Deb, don't lose that card, okay?"

"I won't." I stuffed it into the pocket of the jacket and carried it under one arm, still warm from running, or maybe from my breasts.

We drove home slowly. I said, "Linda, could we get something to eat? I'll pay you back."

She pulled into a drive-in and stopped at the window. "What do you want?"

"Can I have two double burgers and a strawberry shake? And rings?"

"I've seen your stats." She ordered eight, and two shakes.

I ate on the way home. By the time we were halfway there the scarf was tight across my breasts. I drank one shake and most of the other.

She said, "You know why you're so hungry. This is only going to get worse."

"I know." I pictured being trapped on my back by my enormous breasts while Linda and Stacy forced my mouth open and put a pill in. Where was Chloe? Fuck.

Linda said, "Are you okay? I need gas."

I nodded, my mouth full.

She pulled into a gas station and filled the tank. When she put her card in the slot a recorded voice said, "Please see the clerk inside."

Linda said, "I'm sorry, I'll just be a second." She got out and shut her door.

I knew this was the only chance I'd get. By tomorrow I'd be too big to leave, and the next day they'd easily hold me down. I opened the door, silently, and heaved myself upright on the frame.   I picked up the bag with the last two hamburgers, sucked the rest of the shake through the straw, and walked away. Five steps from the car I stopped and went back, and I got the card out of the jacket. I slammed the door again, and the free end of the scarf caught in it. Panicked, I pulled it off my breasts and over my head, and let it drop. The night air flowed over my skin, cool and erotic.

I could see Linda inside, talking to the clerk. I walked quickly to the end of the lot and down the alley. My pants fell partly down and I couldn't spare a hand to hold them up. I wasn't eating enough, and I was losing weight on my hips. I tried not to think about what that meant. I ducked beside a garage and leaned on a parked car to peel them off, working under my breasts blindly but without difficulty.

Headlights shone down the alley as I straightened up. I'd been naked long enough to not be scared. I ducked down in front of the car, and when the lights moved past I stood up, heavily, and followed them. Linda wouldn't double back.

I devoured the burgers as I walked, half bent over, gracelessly, taking huge bites and swallowing them half-chewed, wishing there were more. I knew I needed more food than I could eat. My hands and face were covered in sauce and grease, and it dripped onto my naked breasts. I felt ravenous and feral, hidden by the dark. I crammed rings into my mouth until they were gone, and licked the crumbs out of the paper box, and then I wiped my hands and face on the pants, swabbed my immense soft breasts as far down as I could see, and abandoned them. Wiping grease off myself in a dark alley was a long way from having a hot shower with Chloe to wash my breasts.

I was much further from home than I had been, but it wasn't late, and the traffic was light. For the first while I was light and energetic, excited by the night air and the dark and the way my breasts felt, bouncing gently with each exuberant step. I made good time in the suburb we'd stopped in, wasting energy I couldn't spare, but I didn't care. After half an hour my huge bust started to feel heavy and I breathed harder than I had last night, but I told myself I was okay. When I had to dash across roads I stopped until I'd caught my breath. So far there were endless trees and plants to hide in.

My breasts pointed ahead of me, a bulging pale surface, the narrow line of cleavage absolutely black in the dim light.

Lost in thought, I walked out into a well lighted space between two new trees, barely twelve feet high. A car drove past me and a male voice yelled from the open window, "Hey babeee," and was gone into the night. I dashed back into the shade, my heart pounding, scared again. They'd seen my naked body, but not my impossible breasts. I vowed to keep my back to anyone who might see me. I'd still be naked and have giant boobs. It was a flimsy defense, but all I had.

Fifteen minutes later I came to the edge of the suburb. I crouched for an eternity behind a huge stone and wood sign, hidden and terrified,. When there was no traffic close enough to worry about I dashed across a six lane road against the lights. I took half a dozen steps, fast, and had to slow down as my breasts bounced, massive. I didn't care. I took huge breaths of air, free.

A car pulled up from a side road and onto the one I was crossing, going fast. As it passed me it slowed and a woman yelled, "Slut! Go home to your own man!" Then it was past me, and there was no break in the divided road for it to turn. I ran two hundred yards, faster than ever, and fell into a patch of dark green plants, as tall as my waist. I crouched on hands and knees, panting, for several minutes, saliva dripping in long threads from my open mouth. My breasts swayed back and forth with each deep breath, and my nipples grazed the ground,. A car drove by, slowly, and I was sure it was the same one, but it didn't stop. The woman might have understood and given me a ride, but she was a busybody and I couldn't take that chance.

The next suburb was the same, a mile of houses, but with empty lots where nothing had been built. I skirted them when I could, but not all of the houses had trees, and sometimes I had to cross vacant lots and bare lawns.

I watched lighted windows for human figures. Once a woman looked straight at me and I ran, my breasts bouncing intolerably, panting. Four blocks further on I stopped under a tree, bent over and retched. My breasts hung under me, massively heavy, and I gasped for air. I wondered if the food I'd eaten was already being made into breasts too big to carry, but that was stupid. I straightened up and kept going. My legs were tired and I was thirsty.

Ten minutes further on I crossed the road into the next suburb. A tall wire fence surrounded it, a barrier I couldn't possibly climb. A month ago I'd have gone over it in a few seconds. My breasts pressed into the cold mesh before my fingers found it, keeping me too far away to hang on.

I walked along the front, horribly exposed, sheltered only by intermittent shrubs and weeds. I wanted to go back but I wasn't sure where I was, and my legs were tired. I was out of choices.

I passed a convenience store, walking around the circle of light, brighter than I'd hoped. My breasts glowed like bulging, soft lanterns. Inside, a girl looked at me and picked up the phone. I thought of hiding behind their dumpster, but there was no safety there, and no space for a girl with breasts as big as mine. I had to keep moving.

Five minutes later lights cruised along the main road. I lay face down in a flowerbed behind a patch of exotic plumed grass, wishing my breasts would flatten and not hold me so far away from the black soil, and I silently begged him to go on. A searchlight shone over me and the car drove slowly away.

I struggled to my feet, tired. My breasts were covered in mud, and I was filthy. I stumbled on, only having to lay down twice, and half a mile further on the fence ended. I walked a block off the main road, safer among old houses with big trees and widely spaced streetlights.

Once I set off a motion-sensor alarm, and I ran, bouncing, to the end of the block. A minute later a police car drove past, going back the way I'd come, and another. I dashed for shelter on a porch, knowing that if a light came on I was lost, and huddled in a dark corner, shaking, for several minutes. Just as I crept down the steps another one shot by, but there was a tree between us, with branches down to the ground, and he was going too fast to look around.

I looked under the tree but it was solid with needles and branches. I wondered if I could throw myself on the mercy of an old retired homeowner, but when I straightened up my breasts were freakishly big and heavy. Nobody would let me in. I had to get back to Chloe.

I walked along the pathways by the river and crossed over a bridge. I could have cut through the city and saved time, but I was sure the paths were deserted at night. The end of the bridge was lighted, and

I ducked through the illuminated area and back onto the path. I walked slowly, tired, down the middle of the path.

A man ran past, listening to headphones, and I ducked into the bushes. He'd been under the light and I hadn't.

Half a mile further on a woman caught me in the open. She ran out of the dark and nearly into me, too far from a safe patch of black shadows.

She recoiled. "I'm so sorry. I'm ... you're naked. Are you running? Fuck, what's with your breasts? Are you okay?"

I said, "Yes. I'm on my way home. Please don't tell anyone."

She said, "I should probably call the police."

"No. I'm fine. I have to go." I walked a few steps, and then ran, bouncing hugely, short of air after a hundred yards. If she followed me I couldn't escape. She stood, watching me, and I forced myself not to stop. When I finally couldn't run any further I looked back. She was gone.

A side path led up to the road, and I stumbled up it, spitting out saliva, panting. The traffic was continuous. Fuck. When there was a sparse patch I darted across the road, cradling my breasts in my hands, and between two buildings. A car braked, hard, and someone honked. I hid between three trees, caught my breath, and kept going.

I cut through dark places between tall buildings in the dark, invisible, but aware of how brightly headlights would illuminate my naked skin. I should have been working on a tan, but my breasts hadn't been there long enough to have get one. When I peeked around the next corner they stuck out into the light and glowed brightly, huge orbs, brilliantly lit.

Six blocks took me to Chloe's neighborhood of houses and small apartments, each block studded with signs and trees and bus stops. I could have lived here, an urban sylph, hiding from everyone until daylight showed my impossible glowing breasts to everyone. Fuck.

A car cruised by and I stumbled behind a sign, too tired to really try. He slowed suddenly and turned the corner, and I knew he was coming back. I had twenty seconds. The road was clear for two blocks. I darted across the street and sat down on the grass behind a patch of leafy plants. If anyone came out of the building they'd see me in a second.

The car zoomed round the corner and stopped on the other side of the street, where I'd been. Three men got out and walked into the bushes, calling something. I knew I should sneak away, but I was petrified. One of them looked around, but missed me.

A light came on behind me, and I could see myself haloed in light, my naked back glowing. I threw myself as flat as I could, my breasts enormous firm bulges under me. The front door opened and two couples came out. The men across the street straggled back to their car, embarrassed, and drove away.

I was two blocks from Chloe's place, exhausted. If anyone chased me I couldn't run. My breasts were the biggest thing in the universe, impossibly huge and round and obvious. My nipples shuddered with each tired footstep. I crouched behind a vacancy sign as a car passed, and huddled in a flowerbed for five minutes as a group of partygoers walked drunkenly by. When they were gone I walked after them. There were five lawns with no cover, the worst thing for a terrified night creature. I hesitated, half crouched, looking back and forth. Finally I dashed across the street, panting, into the shelter of two tiny shrubs, and continued down the sidewalk.

A voice yelled, "Hey!"

I broke and ran, dashing frantically around trees and across lawns, leaving footprints in soft soil. Someone said, "Stop!" and I forced myself to go faster, unable to breathe, my thighs burning, completely unsteady. Chloe's house was just ahead, but the footsteps were getting closer. I dashed between the houses and through the open gate into her back yard, and slammed it behind me. I cut across the back of the house and up the other side, finally reduced to a panting walk as someone cursed the gate and kicked it open. I staggered up to the front door, terrified, knowing it would be shut, turned the handle and fell inside. It swung shut behind me.

A tall figure walked up and knocked on the door. I lay in the shadows, not even trying to pant quietly, and he pounded on the glass. I crawled out of the dim light coming through the window, and into the bathroom. The man pounded and yelled, and I bent my head over the toilet and vomited, not caring.

Behind me a light came on. Chloe stood by the door in a housecoat, and yanked it open.

A tall man said, "A girl came in here -"

She spat, "I'm the only girl in here. It's after midnight and I'm trying to sleep. Are you drunk? Get off my porch, asshole!"

"No! I saw a naked girl."

"I'm going to call the cops."

He turned and walked off, cursing.

Chloe shut off the light and came into the bathroom. "Baby, where the hell have you been? Holy fuck, look at your boobs. Can you even stand up?"

I said, "Did you get the antidote?"

"Tomorrow. I'm sure. Come on, let's get you cleaned up. Are you hungry?"

She put me in the bath and asked about where I'd been, and I explained, leaving out seeing Stacy and arguing about the antidote. I'd dropped the card in that last frantic dash, but I was pretty sure I knew where. I told myself I didn't need it.

Chloe's tub was oversized and deep. She filled it until my breasts floated and let me soak. I was blotched with mud all down the front. Probably a few of the times I'd gone unseen were because my outline was broken up, camouflaged with earth. My right breast was dusty but still mostly cream colored, but the left was black with mud and topsoil. I wondered if I could smear myself more thoroughly with mud and be invisible. It didn't matter. There wouldn't be a next time.

Chloe soaped my breasts and washed them, and they bounced up and down under her firm hands. "There. They're too pretty to be dirty." She poured a cup of water over the left one and rubbed it with her fingers. I felt warm and cared for. My boobs stuck up out of the water like a range of two mountains, resting on my chest, so big that they hid the taps and my feet. I breathed out, a sigh that went on longer than it should have. I felt my heart beating, strong but relaxed.

Chloe said, "I'll get you something to eat, and I think we should talk about the antidote." She casually rubbed my right breast, the flesh compressing gently below her spread fingers. "From what I've read it's not as safe as you'd think, and you're not going to get that much bigger."

I froze. The truth I hadn't wanted to accept was crushing me, undeniable. Chloe had no intention of letting me have the antidote. She was my friend, but I was her pet, a creature she could care for and talk to, who had once run rings around her, fun and lively, and who she could now take care of and show off at parties, a prisoner of her own impossible bust.

She stood up. "I'll be right back."

I tried to plan. Chloe doesn't have a land line, and her phone is passworded. I'd lost the card, but I could find it. I couldn't let myself think it was gone. Linda's place wasn't that far, if I went tonight, but Chloe had added oil to the bath water and I wasn't sure I could get out of the smooth, slippery tub. My breasts floated, huge and perfect and useless. I longed to be skinny and fast again, but I knew by tomorrow I'd be bigger, enormously so.

Chloe came back in, carrying a huge bowl of chili. "Here. I know you like this."

I'd decided not to eat, but it smelled delicious and I was famished. I put away three bowls and lay back, stuffed. She brought me a tall glass of milk and I drained it in one shot, horrified and unable to stop.

"Chloe, I want the antidote. I'm getting too big."

"I'm still looking. I'm not sure it's a good idea, but when I find it we can talk. It could be a couple of days."

Why had I been so stupid? I could have taken the antidote and stayed with Linda, or come back here and let Chloe think I'd just stopped growing. I had to escape. "Could I have another glass of milk?" I hated to ask, but I was thirsty.

She brought it and I sat in the bath while she talked about boys and a party she'd been to, people she'd met. There hadn't been time in there for her to look for the antidote, and she didn't mention it.

I couldn't bring it up and let her realize that I knew. We talked of other things, trivial. She brought me dessert, a huge slice of pie with ice cream. I ate it.

At two she said, "It's time for bed."

She'd been letting me get sleepy. No, she'd been letting my breasts grow, sure that even a few hours' growth would make me too heavy to escape. She helped me to my room, my legs stiff and tired, and I could tell she was right. My tits were bigger. The skin felt smooth and tight, and I could feel my nipples bulging out, heavy and thick.

There was a plate of cookies and another glass of milk by my bed. I ate them all and drank the milk. I'd never realized how wonderful it was to drink an entire glass of milk in one delicious shot. Fuck. I was getting too close.

Chloe said, "Another?"

"Please." I drank it even faster, and she looked approving.

"Do you need anything? I'm going to bed, but just call."

"Thanks." I needed her to be asleep, and I'd be gone. I waited until her light was out, and gave her ten minutes. I tried to roll onto my side, but my breasts held me on my back, too big to let me roll over. I was too tired to care. The next thing I knew it was daylight.

Chloe stood by my bed with a plate of food and a jug of milk. "Get up, sleepy. I have to go out."

I struggled to sit up, groggy.

She put the plate on my lap. "I guess you can't see that."

My breasts had swelled enormously. Everyone who'd cared for me yesterday had fed me. I said, "It's okay." I set it off to one side on the bed.

Chloe said, "I'll help." She cut up a sausage and added a slice of egg, dripping with yolk, and held it out to me.

I ate the huge bite. It was very good.

Chloe fed me, quickly and efficiently, interspersing food with milk, not letting me pause.

I said, "Chloe, I can't hold any more."

"Just a few more bites. There, last one. More milk?"

I finished it, too stuffed to get up. She'd intended that. She said, "I have to go out. I'll lock the door, and I'll leave you supper on the stove in case I'm late. Okay?"

I said, "What about clothes?"

"I'll pick you some up. You just stay here. Okay?"

I knew she wouldn't. My breasts stuck out in front of me, fantastically huge.

Chloe eyed them approvingly. "You're getting nice and big."

"You'll get the antidote?"

"Today."

She wouldn't, and by tomorrow I'd be too big to leave, unable to complain. I wondered what she was telling the people we knew. "Deb's getting pretty big. She says 'Hi,' but she can't come out any more." I knew, suddenly, where the pill had come from. She'd found the boy and told him I'd take it. Now she'd go out and be the life of the party, content because she had me waiting at home.

I asked her to help me to the bathroom, and it wasn't an act. I felt like a pyramid balanced on its point, massive and unsteady. When I was back in bed she said, "Take it easy. I'll be back." She covered me with a blanket. My breasts stuck up and loomed above me, impossibly huge. She waved at me over them.

When the door clicked shut I waited, and after a while I dozed. My bladder woke me up in mid-afternoon, and I struggled to my feet. I was terribly heavy, and I clutched the wall to keep from falling over. My breasts bumped into corners and doorframes, immense, and my legs were stiff from last night. I was trapped.

I peed and combed my hair, and I sat at the counter. Chloe had left a huge pot of chili and there was a cheesecake in the fridge, and ice cream in the freezer, half a dozen bags of cookies, and containers of yoghurt. I knew it was a trap. I opened a gallon of milk and drank a third of it, and had a bowl of chili, and another, knowing I'd regret it.

I washed my face in the kitchen sink. Water dripped down and off my breasts, and I dried them as well as I could. I searched my room. The closet held a tiny, tight shirt and a single pair of jeans I couldn't get on. It was a message. Chloe's closet was empty. The top shelf was lined with boxes, but I couldn't reach them. I thought of standing on a chair, but I knew I couldn't possibly do that. I'd never get up, or back down.

I sat at the kitchen counter and thought, ate more chili, sure I could feel the skin on my breasts stretching, and searched the house again. I felt stuffed and heavy, and tired. I sat on the couch and fell asleep.

When I woke up it was getting dark. Chloe wasn't home, and I knew she wouldn't be back until tomorrow. I struggled to my feet, heavily. I was still small and light, except for the giant fat cones that sat on my chest, bulging out in every direction. I went into the bathroom and looked at them in the mirror. They were terrifying, and yet beautiful. My huge nipples capped the furthest part of each enormous peak. I could only see them in the mirror. When I reached up, amazed, to touch them, my hands looked lost on the huge curves.

I pulled her small scale out from under the counter with my toes, and I stood on it and heard the springs creak, but there was no way I could read the number. I didn't want to know.

Stacy had said I had to eat, but I knew each bite meant bigger boobs. I sat and looked at the chili for half an hour, then ate a bowl, and two more, leaving myself full and awkward. I finished the gallon of milk.

I stared down at the floor, a place completely out of my reach. I picked the spoon out of my bowl and dropped it, deliberately. It bounced three feet, ringing, and stopped.

I got down to my knees, holding the counter, and then bent carefully over and stretched my free hand out until I could almost reach the floor, let go and fell heavily to all fours, my breasts hitting the black and white tiles. They pressed heavily into my arms and when I tried to crawl they bumped into my thighs, swinging back and forth massively. I reached beneath them, beneath *myself*, and was relieved to find the thickness of a finger between my nipples and the floor.

I reached the spoon and picked it up, and had nowhere to put it. I tried to stuff it in my cleavage, but you don't really have that unless you're wearing a bra, and I was sure I'd never put one on again. I didn't miss them, but for a while they'd been cute and sexy. I hadn't got laid while I'd had merely big boobs, and now it was too late. I wondered if Chloe would let me have a lover.

I held the spoon in my mouth and tried to rear up, but I couldn't. Fuck. I was trying to escape, and now I was scared Chloe would come back and find me stuck on the floor, undignified, making our awful power imbalance even worse.

I'd always assumed that even if I couldn't stand up I could crawl, but this was impossible. I crept along in tiny increments, my breasts banging softly into my thighs and arms. When I made it to the counter I reached up and grabbed the edge and pulled myself upright. My breasts squashed into it, enormous, much too heavy to lift.

I lunged up, my thigh muscles screaming, and fell across the counter just before they gave out. My breasts rested immensely on it, the smooth granite cool against their metabolic warmth. I forced myself to stand straight up, lifting their weight off the counter. I was massively top-heavy, but I could move.

The microwave clock was flashing 12:00. Chloe hadn't wanted me to know what time it was, but that didn't matter. It was dark. I sat on the couch by the window, my breasts resting on my lap, and watched the traffic. Twice I got up and ate chili and yoghurt, and I peed, finding my way in the bathroom by touch. Everything was below my breasts, hidden.

An unknown time later I started to feel antsy. Chloe isn't really a party creature, not without me, and she'd come home when she was sure I'd be asleep or immobile. The traffic was dying down, and it was pitch black. Not even a sliver of the moon showed above the horizon. I didn't have to make it to Linda's place, but I had to get out of here.

I ate another plate of food and drank half a gallon of milk. It went down too easily, cold and wonderful, quenching the heat inside me. It was easy to stand up off the stool, even though my breasts felt heavier. I peed, washed my face, dried myself and the enormous upper curves of my breasts, and went to the front door.

Five cars went past while I waited in the dark. I thought about getting more food, but I'd eaten too much, and I was stuffed and heavy.

I opened it a crack and looked out. Off in the distance a car headed towards me, but they were too far away to see me, to make my tiny figure into a naked girl with impossibly big tits. I stepped out and shut the door.

Faced with the huge open space and the dark sky I was immobile, lost. I walked heavily, and I could tell my breasts now weighed more than the rest of me. My hands extended themselves for balance. This was impossible. I couldn't run, and if I had to duck down I'd be too heavy to stand up. I studied the path between the houses. My breasts bulged hugely up in front of me. I wouldn't be able to see it over them when I got close to curbs and steps. The car was nearly here. I stepped between the houses.

It slowed, pulled into the driveway and stopped. Chloe got out, carrying a case of beer, and went up to the house.

As the door shut I tried to dash, but I could only walk at a slow, heavy pace, breasts wobbling and swaying. My nipples were hugely erect because I was naked and it was dark and cool out, and for the first time in days I felt good, free. The neighbors had a stand of tall trees, conifers, and I pushed into the dark space between them and waited. I'd have dashed across the street, but roads are a terrifying chasm when you're naked and scared and too top-heavy to go fast.

Lights came on in the house and I watched Chloe dash from room to room. I waited, my heart pounding, breathing hard, and she came out and called, "Deb! I have the antidote! I got it."

It was a lie. If she could trick me into staying one more night she'd have me. She went back in, leaving the lights on, and came back out. I heard car keys jingle and the engine start, and I was safe. She couldn't see anything but her headlights.

The car drove around the block and away into the dark. My massive breasts pushed branches aside, needles scraped my pale skin, and I was out.

A car drove past, but it wasn't Chloe. I stood between two trees, half exposed, but they didn't see me in the shadow. I planned my route to the next house and walked across the lawn, my feet sinking heavily into the soft grass.

Two blocks later I'd seen no-one. I was breathing heavily and my heart was beating a bit fast, but I was okay. I stopped to lean on an ornamental boulder, and a car turned the corner, accelerating too fast. I ducked to hands and knees and crouched down, resting my breasts on the soft earth. Chloe zoomed past, looking frantic.

The ground was comfortable and cool, and I wanted to stay there, but daylight wasn't that many hours away. I felt like a hunted creature.

I pulled myself upright, the rock scraping past my nipples, rough but not unpleasant or painful. When I was sure I was steady I walked as lightly as I could to the end of the block, checked for cars, and trotted across the street. My breasts bounced, liquidly soft but firm. I made it into the shade of the first house, breathing hard.

Halfway down the block a sprinkler sprayed a lawn and a flowerbed. I wanted it, desperately. Two cars drove past while I walked from shadow to tree. Once I had to stop and crawl, and it was incredibly slow. I was afraid I wouldn't be able to get up, but I just made it.

I passed a dark window, and a small girl looked out at me with huge eyes. I smiled and waved. If she called her parents I was gone, but I knew she wouldn't. She waved back.

I reached the sprinkler and tried to drink from it, but the tiny jets were too small. I gripped the hose connection and twisted, and it came apart, corroded and stiff, but okay. I drank until I was chilled and I could feel water sloshing inside me, terrified, not able to stop. Water was amazing. I felt my breasts swell with the wonderful liquid and my nipples stuck out further. I forced myself to drop the hose.

I bent over, my breasts massively heavy and full, and picked up a handful of wet earth from the edge of the flowerbed. It was cold and thick. I looked at it for a minute, but there were lights coming. I filled both hands, cupped my right breast and smeared the black goo all over it, letting it stick, picked up another handful and forced it into my cleavage, and did my belly and my legs.

I couldn't do my back. I was too far gone to quit. I sat, heavily, and then lay down in the cold mud, and squirmed around, rolling over and trying to coat myself, making sure it filled my pubic hair and my the space between my cheeks, smearing my underarms and finally kneeling to do my face. My hair was full of mud and matted, and I made it worse and let it hang over my face. When looked down I couldn't see anything but mud. I picked up a double handful and smeared my belly and the underside of my breasts, again. I knelt up, sliding in the mud, but I didn't care. I smeared the backs of my knees and the insides of my thighs. Then I clambered to my feet, heavy and wet and cold, and went on.

I walked along, not caring, for half a mile. When cars drove by I stepped behind a tree, if there was one, or knelt behind a flowerbed. I hated having to dirty my skin with mud, but it was worth it to be invisible. Once I waited twenty minutes for a break in traffic, knowing I couldn't run. I needed to pee, badly, but I couldn't chance washing off any mud.

On the next road I cut it too close. I was stiff from last night, and chunks of dried mud were flaking off. I knew this wouldn't last forever. The nearest car was three blocks away, too close, and one had just passed. I stepped out into the road and walked across, quickly.

The car ahead of me was nearly at the corner when its taillights came on and it slowed. A moment later it pulled to the right and turned, hit the curb, backed up, and came after me.

I was already running. My breasts were too heavy and my legs tired, and that didn't matter at all. My body pumped adrenalin into my veins and I ran, bouncing and panting.

On the other side of the road was a bare lawn. I ran across it. My legs were on fire, and I couldn't get enough air, but I ran to the next one, ignored a stand of shrubs because I needed something better, and finally, on the next one, saw a gate into a back yard and a garden shed with an open door. I struggled to it, clutching my breasts, enormously too big, too panicked to care if I wiped off the dried, flaking mud. I dashed inside and sat on the floor, huddled behind a lawnmower. I couldn't stop panting, and my heart pounded.

Car doors slammed and feet ran up a sidewalk and then across the lawn. Someone said, a girl, "This way."

I heard footsteps run into the back yard, endlessly faster and more agile than me. A small shape was silhouetted in the doorway. I forced myself to hold my breath, in agony.

Someone said, "Anything?"

"Nope, garden tools." She turned away.

I waited. Someone said, "The gate's open."

"I'll get the car." They ran off in two directions. I stuck my head out of the door, scared that it was a trap, but the car pulled ahead. Its lights washed past, never directly touching me.

I felt trapped in the tiny space. Being outside was scary, but there was an escape route, usually. I stepped out and stood close to the dark, quiet house. Nothing moved. I tiptoed down to the alley.

In the dark I was invisible again. I walked down silent, dark alleys, my calves on fire when I used my toes to absorb the shocks that made my breasts shake, sometimes landing hard on my heels and not caring.

The street at the end of the block was empty and silent. I walked along it until I was across from the next alley, looked around like a wild creature waiting for predators, then trotted across it as quickly as I could.

A car turned the corner, but I was back in the shadows. I ducked beside a garage and waited. They drove past. I heard music playing through their windows, part of a world I'd lost.

Halfway down the next alley a voice said, "Hey!"

I froze.

"I can see you. Come here!"

I turned and ran, pounding heavily on the gravel. Footsteps followed me for half a dozen steps and gave up. I cut across another block, afraid that he'd called the cops, but the night was still.

At the next street I crouched in a flowerbed, conscious of my failing disguise. My knees and hands were mostly bare, and the mud had mostly peeled off my right breast. I could feel air on my nipples. I squatted, carefully, and peed. A break appeared in the traffic but I couldn't stop. When I was finished I crawled ten feet, away from the wet area. My breasts hung below me and stuck out to the sides, wider than my body. I could feel the skin tensing as the enormous globes pulled down, and my thighs squashed them forwards into my arms. I realized, horrified, that my nipples were resting lightly on the ground. I tried not to worry, and concentrated on the traffic.

There was another break, not a safe one, but I was too tired. I stood up, patched with mud and filthy skin, and walked across, limping slightly. A car honked and I ignored it. I found a patch of trees on the first lawn. They kept going.

I tried to figure out where I was. I was fairly sure I didn't have too many blocks to go, but I'd walked into a small shopping district and my coating of mud made me more noticeable than if I'd only been naked and impossibly busty.

I moved from doorway to doorway, hoping nobody would see me if I stayed in the shadows. Once I crouched behind a battered newspaper box while cars went by, and dashed as fast as I could to a pile of garbage by the curb.

I wasted five minutes going down a dead-end alley, sure it would get me further along. Just as the solid end wall stopped me I heard a door open between me and the street. I crouched down, tense and scared, and watched two men in stained white cook's outfits come out and light cigarettes. I looked up past the top of the buildings for any sign of daylight, but the sky was still dark. I had no idea what time it was, and I cursed Chloe. After an endless time the cooks went back in. I dashed past their door, breathing hard. I had to force myself to step out of the minimal safety of the alley and onto the street.

A police car drove past. I knelt in an unlighted doorway and draped my filthy hair over my face. He kept going. A man walked out of a building with a dog on a leash, heading the other way. It turned and pulled towards me, growling, but he yanked it back on course and didn't glance at me.

The final block was bare and brightly lit. I crossed to the other side of the street to find a trivial amount of cover, begrudging the time and distance, exhausted and tense. Two cars ignored me. Traffic was picking up.

I struggled slowly along the last fifty yards. Twice I grazed my right breast along the concrete wall. I forced myself not to clutch them, then gave up. Under my spread fingers they were enormous, bigger than I'd imagined I could lift.

A car braked beside me and a window rolled down. "Hey! Filthy guy!"

I ran twenty yards, using energy I didn't have, pulled the door open and stepped inside. A car door slammed and I pushed mine shut and tipped over the flyer box in front of it.

A figure shoved at it and cursed, and the door banged into the metal box. I was already at the door to the stairs. I heard the elevator chime and someone yelled, but I was gone.

The first flight was torture, and each one after it was worse. I took them a step at a time, leaning against the wall, my heart pounding, terrified that someone would come up and catch me, easily. I turned onto the second flight, my legs already shaky and exhausted, and I heard the lobby door open at the bottom. I stood, frozen, but nobody came. I climbed the next three flights increasingly slowly, four steps and a break, then two, and one. I lifted each foot, slowly, and rested before I used the railing to pull myself up onto the next step. All I could see was concrete stairs and the top of two enormous breasts, the skin smooth and pale where dried mud had fallen off them and gathered in dry brown flakes in my cleavage. I took the last two one step at a time, my legs cramping, sobbing in frustration.

At the top I rested for a long time before I tried to pull myself upright. I had the railing to hang on to, and I barely made it. I stumbled through the door and over to my old place, Linda's place, afraid I'd leave a trail of mud, but I was almost clean below my knees. I tried not to let my breasts touch the door as I reached up for the key. They were impossibly too big and they squashed into it, leaving dusty impressions. I didn't care.

The key was gone. I was finished, trapped, probably dead. I wanted to scream and cry, but nothing happened. I stood, silent and lost. There was nothing else to do.

My breasts pressed against the door. Sticking out above the left one was a note. I leaned back and read it.

Deb. It's open. Come in.

The elevator dinged. I turned the knob and stepped in. Voices talked outside, but they didn't matter. I locked the door and leaned against it, sobbing, and I slowly slid down to the floor.

A light came on in the corridor and Linda was there, doing up the belt on a pale blue housecoat. "Who are ... oh! Deb! What happened? Come on, we have to get you in the bath." I struggled erect, my legs shaking, and she half supported me. She turned on the shower and ran a bath at the same time.

I reached for the clothes I wasn't wearing, stupid with fatigue, and got under the stream of hot water. Linda held the hose and rinsed soil off me, leaving a layer of mud half an inch thick on the tiled floor. Her refusal to help me in the shower had evaporated now I was filthy and distressed. I stood, unable to speak, and concentrated on being warm and safe.

She shut the taps off. "Okay, get in the bath."

I sat in deep, hot water and leaned forward so my breasts floated, and Linda rubbed soap all over me, sluicing away the last film of grey, making my skin its proper pink color. She said, "Deb, tell me what's going on."

I talked as she washed me, sometimes sobbing with fatigue and fear and frustration. I explained how I'd realized she was right about Chloe, and how I was suddenly thirsty, and knowing I was too big to escape, but having to, and my desperate flight over here, and realizing how enormous my breasts were, and that I should have found the antidote myself, as soon as I knew, or have never taken the pill in the first place.

Linda poured shampoo on my head and rubbed it into lather, rinsed me with a plastic bowl, and let the water out. "It's okay, you're here now."

I looked down at my breasts, floating serenely, squashed sideways to fit in the bath. "But it's not. I'm still like *this*."

She rinsed the last mud and grit down the drain and put the plug in. "Let's deal with that first." She took out her phone and dialed. "Stacy? Yeah, I'm sorry. I need you over here, now. No, it's Deb. Yes. Bye."

Stacy arrived half an hour later.

I was sitting at the kitchen table with a big mug of tea while Linda untangled my hair.

Stacy gasped, and I realized I was still naked. She said, "No. Deb? *One day?*"

Linda said, "Did you bring it?"

She pulled a small case out of her pocket. "We can't do it if she's at the tipping point." She turned to me. "Deb, are you thirsty?"

"A little."

She found a gallon of milk in Linda's fridge and put it in front of me. "Drink as much as you like."

I tilted it up and drank, not stopping until I couldn't go on and there were trickles, whiter than my breasts, running down them.

"Thanks." There was half an inch in the bottom.

Stacy sighed. "I think we're okay. She's really close. I brought the injectable form. Deb, are you ready?"

I hesitated. "Stacy, are you sure?"

"Yes. If I don't inject you with this, now, you'll be too big to move by tomorrow night, and dead in a month. I can't see how you walked here."

Linda said, "Her spine is a mass of muscle. It's a new version of the treatment."

I said, "So I could be all right?"

Stacy shook her head. "No. *Listen.* I've got another girl, Belinda. She's dead."

"When?" Linda was shocked.

"Today."

I asked, "How?"

"Nothing sexy or romantic. All of her systems failed. She couldn't drink enough to keep up, or eat enough. She couldn't stand, her breasts were like beach balls, and her heart couldn't pump enough blood. They just kept getting bigger, and she wasted away. She was like a skeleton with enormous tits. We put about twenty IVs into her, and her electrolyte balance went wrong, and her liver started to fail. Her heart was stuck at about a hundred and ninety beats a minute, and she started convulsing. It wasn't pretty."

"And she was like me?"

"No. You're bigger, and you'll die faster. If you don't take this I'll do it anyway. I don't care." She opened the case and took out a small syringe with a short needle.

Linda said, "Wait. Deb, you've only got a few hours. You have to decide now. If you don't do this you'll die in a few days."

I said, "Why didn't they cut off her boobs?"

Stacy said, "She wouldn't let us, and by the end she wouldn't have survived the surgery. All of her systems were failing." She wiped her eyes. "She was my friend. I knew her. She kept saying, 'But Stacy, they're so pretty.'" She swung her hand and drove the needle into my right breast, as far as it would go, and pushed the plunger home. "There. Now you won't die. It'll take a few hours to work, but if you're lucky you'll be okay." She pulled it out and tossed it in the open trash can.

Linda said, "Stacy, you should have let her decide for herself."

"No." I rubbed my breast. "She's right. I wouldn't ever have done it." I stared down into my hot chocolate. "What now?"

"We watch you, because you still might tip over. If you do we have to get about twenty gallons of liquid into you, and as much food as you can take, and we have to get you into a pool. Then we'll see how long we can keep you alive."

I said, "I think if that happens you should ... do the surgery."

She screwed up her face. "You're the next improvement. I think they changed your body to make that impossible." She rummaged in her bag. "We just got this." She set a small box on the table and unrolled a screen. "Hold still."

Nothing happened for a minute, and she said, "Okay."

"What?"

"I scanned you. Your heart rate is high, but it's steady. You're breathing okay. Liver functions look good. I think you're all right."

I sighed, relieved. "So this is it?"

"No. You'll get bigger for another twelve hours, maybe sixteen, and you'll be ravenous. It'll taper off, and we'll see if you can stand up. You'll have to avoid anything that might encourage your breasts to lactate, for at least six months, and you'll need someone to take care of you." She looked up at me. "I'm sorry, Deb. You can't live by yourself. You're just too big. You should watch your weight, too. You're naturally skinny, but you don't know about the DNA that did this to you, and you can't afford to be any bigger."

"I know." I wished Linda would wash my hair when I needed it, and let me live here, but now I wasn't filthy and sobbing she'd pulled away. "So Chloe's out of the question."

They exchanged glances.

Linda said, "Chloe is your best choice."

"What?!"

Stacy said, "Chloe came over today, after you disappeared. She was looking for you, and she was very upset. I got her to do some psychological tests."

"And she's insane?"

"No. She's pretty realistic, but she has a knot of fetishes I don't want to try and untangle. She loves you, you know."

"Huh? Chloe?"

"She's in love with you. It's not that uncommon. She wants to take care of you, and for you to need her, but she also looks up to you and wants you two to have fun and get into trouble."

I said, "She's pretty much put an end to that." My breasts rested on the table, moving slightly when I breathed.

"She's certain you'll think of something." Stacy shrugged. "Bear in mind, this won't be a normal relationship. She'll go on screwing guys, but the only relationship that will last is with you. If you're jealous at all this won't work."

"I can handle that, if I can have boys, too." I studied my breasts. They were round and perfect, and I secretly thought they were beautiful. I laid my hand on one and pressed, the firm flesh, soft and slightly warmer than my hand. "If any boy wants me, and if I can learn to fuck with these things."

Linda said, "Belinda was pretty successful before she got too sick. She left some notes, too. About living with them, and what she thought, but also about making love with huge boobs. I'll give them to you."

"What about the pills? She could feed me another one."

Stacy tossed the empty vial in the trash. "You're safe. She promised us she wouldn't. The antidote makes you immune to the phages that carry the updated genetics. I didn't tell her that."

I nodded. "Thanks."

We sat up through the night. At around four Linda made a huge breakfast, and I ate almost all of it. Stacy scanned me again and didn't say anything. She shook her head at Linda, once.

We ate again as it got light. Linda made tea, and when she set the milk down I finished it, and most of her next gallon.

Stacy looked alarmed, scanned me again, and relaxed.

I said, "Okay?" I was too tired to care, exhausted by the last few days. If I had milk, that would be nice, and I'd deal with it.

"I think so. You're closer to lactating than any other girl I've seen. Bigger, too."

My breasts were swelling, getting fuller and heavier. When I moved they wobbled on the table. I was sure they were bigger around. I couldn't see the chair on the other side over them.

I fell asleep at around seven o'clock, leaning into my breasts, my face resting on the right one. Linda woke me up and helped me to her spare bed. She lifted me to my feet, and if she hadn't been there

I'd have fallen over twice. I slept for ten hours.

It was still light when I woke up. I was lying on my back, my breasts looming over me, impossibly big. They felt immensely heavy, but warm and comfortable.

Stacy stood on the other side of them. Linda was with her, holding a tray. She set it on the bedside table and sat down on the mattress, beside me. "Deb? Don't panic, all right? You're okay, but you won't be able to sit up by yourself, or stand up. Stacy and I will help you, and we'll figure out what to do from here." She smiled. "Your boobs are a lot bigger, but you're still alive."

I felt blurry and groggy, but my thoughts were clear. I leaned up and my breasts swayed on my chest, soft and warm and enormously heavy. I tried to get my hands up beside me but they were trapped. I struggled to get free, and I realized I was thrashing frantically, yelling in frustration.

Stacy put her hands on my shoulders. "Deb! Calm down, we'll help. Stop! You'll hurt yourself."

I said, angrily, "I just want to sit up!" I managed to pull my right arm free, and then my left, and I put my palms flat on the mattress, but I couldn't lift myself.

"Wait." Stacy grabbed my right arm and put a hand under my back, and Linda did the same on my right. For a moment I'd thought she was going to grab my right breast and lift it for me, but she didn't. I was terribly heavy, but I didn't mind. I tensed my stomach muscles and leaned up, and they helped, and I sat up. I managed to shuffle back to lean on the headboard, pushing with my legs. My breasts rested on my lap, enormous, but I could see over them.

Stacy said, "There."

I struggled to sit straight up so I could see more of the room, and managed to raise my chin above their vast, gentle curves.

Linda let go of my arm. "That wasn't too bad." She smiled encouragingly. She thought I'd spend my life sitting up in bed. I didn't reply.

Stacy was holding her scanner. "Hold still, honey."

I wanted to say I wasn't going to get up and dance around, but I nodded.

She said, "Good. Your breasts are still getting bigger, but it's tapering off. I don't think you're going to have milk." She studied her screen and read it. "You're a beautiful shape, and very firm. If your breasts were spheres, they'd be a bit more than seventeen inches in diameter. Maybe seventeen and a half. They weigh just over a hundred pounds each."

Linda looked worried. "We don't think you should try to get up. It's impossible, and your legs and back aren't strong enough. I think with therapy you can learn to stand, and you might eventually be able to take a few steps without help, but that's all. I'm sorry."

I nodded. "Could I be alone for a minute?"

Linda said, "Do you want me to feed you? I don't mind."

"No, that's okay. I just need to think."

They left, and Linda shut the door. I could hear them talking outside. I ran my hands over my breasts. They were beautiful, and I told myself that was what this had been about. I'd got what the boy with the pills had promised. I leaned forward, pressing my arms into the soft curves and managed to stretch just far enough to touch the outer edge of my nipples.

I was famished. I balanced the plate on my left breast and held it steady with my left hand while I ate with my right. It sat firmly on the big, gentle curve. Halfway through I switched, so I could practice using my left hand. My breasts were always going to be in the way, and I had to learn to deal with that.

When I was finished I used the blunt knife to scrape the spilled food off my breasts and out of my cleavage. I called for Linda and she brought me a bedpan. I peed, hating the indignity, until it nearly overflowed.

Linda wiped my breasts with a damp cloth. "Deb, Chloe is here. She wants to talk. I told her I'd ask if you were up to that."

I said, "Okay."

She opened the door and said something, and she stepped outside.

Stacy came in and ran her scanner over me. "You're okay so far. They'll grow a bit more, but right now you're safe." She closed it up, smiled at me, and left.

Chloe had come in, and she stood by the door, silent, until we were alone. She closed the door behind Stacy and spoke, not happy. "I guess I'm the bad guy. I tried to kill my friend." She sat on the bed beside me and said, "I'm sorry." She leaned over to hug me, but my breasts were in the way, enormous. I tried not to think that they were bigger than the rest of me. I reminded myself that they were me, and they were beautiful.

She crushed both of her smaller breasts into mine and leaned over. "I'm so sorry." She burst into tears, hugging my bust more than me.

I didn't mind. I said, "They're awfully nice."

"They're gorgeous, in an insane way."

I said "I need someone to take care of me."

She sniffed. "I'd do that." Her face screwed up again. "I didn't want you to be stuck like this. I'm sorry."

I said, "Do you love me?"

She looked up and wiped her eyes. Tears ran down my breast, tickling my skin. "No. It's not like that."

I said, "I want to be with you, forever. You can fuck all the boys you want, but you have to stay with me. Because I love you."

She nodded. "Even though I did this to you?"

"You just wanted to keep me."

She wiped her face. "Will you come home? We'll get a shopping cart or something."

"Yes." I ran my fingers through the tears on my breasts, and reached up to mix them with the ones running down her face. "Don't cry. We'll have fun."

"How?!" It was an anguished wail. "I've ruined everything!"

I said, "Chloe, promise me something. If I say a thing is important, you'll do it, no matter what. If I'm going to be like this, you have to promise, and mean it."

Tears welled up in her eyes and overflowed. She sobbed, "I promise."

I nodded, and I said, "I'm tired. Can I be alone for a while?"

"Are you comfortable? I can help you move around. Do you want me to cover your boobs?"

The last thing I wanted was to make them look bigger, and they were still warm enough. "No. Just let me be. I'll yell."

She nodded and left me lying there, helpless under the weight of my breasts. They lay on my chest, enormously heavy and inert, and I sat and watched them rise and fall with my breathing. My heart beat powerfully and fast, but it was slowing down as my body adapted to them.

I waited until they'd all had time to settle down. I knew Linda and Stacy wouldn't be awake long. They hadn't slept since last night.

When I was sure enough time had passed I put my hands by my

sides and pushed myself as upright as I could, lifted my breasts off my legs and my lap, and straightened up, lifting them massively into the air. They were terribly, impossibly heavy, but I was already getting used to that. I swiveled round and put my legs over the edge and found the rug with my feet. I caught myself and leaned forward to make sure the floor was clear. I wouldn't be able to see anything standing up.

I took a deep breath and leaned forwards. My nipples slid over my knees and hung off into space. When my centre of gravity was above my feet and my breasts were trying to pull me over forward I grabbed the headboard on one side and the bed on the other, and straightened my back and my knees. The bed creaked ominously, and my muscles weren't strong enough. I teetered forward, not quite able to straighten my legs. I knew that if I fell onto my hands and knees the weight of my breasts would hold me and I'd never be able to get up. My hand clutched the headboard and I stopped, a fraction of an inch away from falling forward, but I was standing. I forced my screaming thighs to pull me upright.

My breasts rose before me, blocking out most of the room. I didn't care. They were round and flawless, and I still thought they were sexy. The cool night air came in the open window and blew over my areolas, by now bigger than I could span with my spread fingers, and my nipples popped out, erect.

I steadied myself and took a deep breath to relax. My balance wasn't right. I realized my center of gravity had moved forward as my bust got bigger. Now it was just in front of where my breasts met my ribcage, and instead of my weight being balanced over my whole feet it had moved forward and was just behind my toes. I stood up perfectly straight and moved my weight over the balls of my feet, trying to adapt to it being forward of where instinct told me it should be.

I felt strangely light and agile. I balanced heavily on one foot and felt ahead of me with the other, making sure the floor was clear. I took a step and another, and my breasts pulled me over forward, slowly and then faster. I'd screwed up, been too confident. I tried to catch myself, but by immense bust was far too heavy. The wall loomed up and my breasts both hit it at the same time. The whole room seemed to vibrate, and then everything was still. I was leaning over at an angle, my breasts gently squashed between my chest and the wall. I felt idiotic, but I was okay.

I pushed myself upright and got my balance again, this time much more carefully. That had almost been catastrophic, and I had no margin of error at all. Eventually I'd learn to get up off the floor, and be strong enough, but that would take time.

I took tiny steps, at first no more than an inch, and I made sure I was perfectly balanced after each one, before I took the next. Walking wasn't a continuous thing. I planned each tiny step, balancing like a tightrope walker, and steadied myself after it.

I glimpsed myself in Linda's big mirror, enormous and unsteady but I thought I looked strangely elegant, my arms spread out to the sides for balance, fingers splayed out and elbows slightly bent, almost on tiptoes. I placed my foot gently, making sure the floor was clear before I was too far forward to pull back, took another step and teetered, insanely top-heavy, scared. Several times I turned sideways to make sure I knew where the furniture was.

It took me an hour to learn to walk without being terrified, and fifteen minutes to cross the room to the attached bathroom. My breasts were too wide for the doorway, but I angled in sideways. The light switch was too low down, hidden behind my breasts, but I realized that the light wouldn't help at all. Everything in the small room was over the horizon of my bust.

I felt around, moving my feet as slowly as I could, and found the toilet. When I was sitting down I could see the sink and bath. I relieved myself, happy not to need a bedpan again, washed my face and dried it and my breasts. I'd have showered but I was sure breasts wouldn't fit inside the tiny stall. I'd probably never bathe again without Chloe. I didn't mind.

I went back into the bedroom and practiced walking, and I sat down on the bed and got up again, twice. It was very hard, but I did it both times. Then I sat again, and planned what I had to say.

I hadn't thought about opening the door. I nearly fell over fumbling for the handle, and when I stood close enough to find it, my breasts were pressed into the door so I couldn't pull it towards me. I stood off to the right, my nipples pressed into the wall, and opened it backwards with my left hand.

I walked down the short corridor and into the open area, trying to look confident. Linda was asleep in the armchair, and Stacy was stretched out on a couch. Chloe leaned back on the other, her eyes closed.

I walked over to her. "Chloe."

She didn't move. I couldn't lean down and shake her. She was right beside me but too far down, out of reach. I put my right hand on the back of the couch, leaned forward with infinite caution, and reached my left around my breasts to ruffle her hair.

She started. "What?!"

I straightened up, almost easily. "Chloe. Come in the bedroom."

"Huh?" She rubbed sleep out of her eyes and stood up. "Deb, you can't stand up."

Linda stirred and relaxed.

I whispered, "Hush. Let them sleep." I took her into the bedroom, walking slowly but with more confidence. She walked amazingly fast, as though it was nothing, and waited for me, patient.

I said, "Chloe, we're going home. You and I."

She looked happy. "You forgive me?"

"You made a promise. If you'll keep your word I'll forgive you. If not I'll stay here and get someone professional to take care of me. I'll hate it, but if you won't keep your promise I can't stay with you."

She straightened up. "All right. If you say it's important I'll do it."

"Good. You and I are walking home."

"Deb, it's about five miles."

"It's two. I've walked it three times."

"You were nowhere near this big."

"I was nearly this big, and I was naked."

She looked at me with wide eyes. "Deb. No."

"It's important to me. I'm slow, and you're skinny and fast. You have to be beside me, and if someone sees me you have to run interference."

"*Naked?*"

"Yes. You have to get their attention and draw them away. Chloe, I can't possibly run, and if anyone sees us you'll have to protect me."

She looked at me, speechless, for a long time. Then she nodded, bent down and undid her pants and stepped out of them, pulled her blouse over her head, and ditched her bra. She was taller than me, and not quite as skinny, with large, firm breasts. They'd have been a nice size if I hadn't been standing there, impossibly bigger. "Let's go." She kicked the discarded clothing under the bed.

We walked to the door, slowly, and waited for an elevator. It stopped on the fifth floor and a woman got in. Chloe met her astonished stare and she looked away. After a few seconds her eyes dropped to my cleavage and stayed there. I could hear her breathing.

At the front door Chloe stepped outside and stopped to check out the street. I'd have ducked into the shadows, but she strolled across the road and turned down the sidewalk, casually staying in the less lighted areas, but not going out of her way to hide.

I said, "Chloe, slow down."

"Oops, sorry, Deb. What are you going to do when we get home?"

I padded after her, a skinny girl following a pair of enormous pointed breasts, trying to stay in the shadows while her more brazen friend strode along in the light, her long dark hair streaming behind her. I knew Chloe, but I'd never seen her like this before. She wasn't covering for me, she just naturally didn't care who saw her.

She glanced at me. "Are you doing okay?"

I said, "Yes. When we get home I'm going to have a shower, and you'll help me, and then I'll sleep. Tomorrow night I'm going to sit in a club wearing a tight shirt, and when enough boys have piled up around me I'm going to pick one and fuck him senseless. Maybe all of them. Then I'll go home to bed."

"Alone?"

"No, you'll be there."

A car cruised past and she glared at it. "I'll do the same. You can bring one home if you like. I don't mind. Just so long as you don't go away with him."

I said, "Is that very important?"

"Yes."

"Then it's a deal." I was getting the hang of this, and if I fell over she'd help me get up. I said, "Let's go," and walked almost quickly. My breasts, warm and soft, bounced heavily in front of me.

I knew something I hadn't told anyone else. I was getting milk. I could feel my breasts swelling, getting ready, and I'd soon need to drink gallons of water, but not yet. I was breathing deeply, and I could my heart beating, more powerful than it had been. Linda hadn't understood. Whoever had made the drug I'd taken had fixed the problems it caused, and I'd be all right.

I'd need to be milked, but that was okay. Chloe would nurse from my breasts. She'd be unable to resist. I'd have a line of boys, each ready to nurse, and women, too. Chloe would always be first. I pictured her, milk-fed and plump, unable to resist me, and I knew that I'd be her pet, her domestic cow, but I'd be in charge, and I'd have dozens of them, all desperate for my milk, unable to refuse me, to escape.

Chloe turned to see me, her eyes bright in the dark. My breasts were enormously heavy, and I could feel her watching them.

I felt confident, satisfied, milky, and I knew I'd be dripping when we got home. She'd find me boys to nurse, because I'd ask, and she'd promised.

She asked, "Are you okay? I'm not going too fast?"

"I'm fine. This is great."

She hugged me over my immense soft bust, awkward. "It is. Let's go."

www.ingramcontent.com/pod-product-compliance
Lightning Source LLC
Chambersburg PA
CBHW072124150726
47999CB00005B/2111